ELEMENTS OF GENIUS

GENIUS

NIKKI TESLA
AND THE FELLOWSHIP
OF THE BLING

ALSO BY JESS KEATING

Nikki Tesla and the Ferret-Proof Death Ray

ELEMENTS OF GENIUS

NIKKI TESLA AND THE FELLOWSHIP OF THE BLING

JESS KEATING
ILLUSTRATED BY LISSY MARLIN

SCHOLASTIC PRESS

NEW YORK

Library of Congress Cataloging-in-Publication Data
Names: Keating, Jess, author. | Keating, Jess. Elements of genius; 2.
Title: Nikki Tesla and the fellowship of the bling / Jess Keating.
Description: First edition. | New York: Scholastic Press, 2020. | Series:
Elements of Genius; 2 | Audience: Ages 8–12. | Audience: Grade 4 to 6. |
Summary: When Mary Shelley is kidnapped by a mad scientist, Nikki
Tesla and the other members of the Genius Academy team are forced to
agree to steal a priceless, lethal high-tech ring in order to free her; but
Nikki also plans to use the heist to get closer to her long-lost father
who claims he is not the criminal mastermind she believes him to be.
Identifiers: LCCN 2019025338 (print) | LCCN 2019025339 (ebook) |
ISBN 9781338295252 (hardcover) | ISBN 9781338295276 (ebook)
Subjects: LCSH: Gifted persons—Juvenile fiction. | Private schools—
Juvenile fiction. | Inventions—Juvenile fiction. | Theft—Juvenile
fiction. | Fathers and daughters—Juvenile fiction. | Kidnapping—
Juvenile fiction. | Adventure stories. | CYAC: Genius—Fiction. | Gifted
children—Fiction. | Schools—Fiction. | Inventions—Fiction. |
Stealing—Fiction. | Fathers and daughters—Fiction. | Kidnapping—
Fiction. | Adventure and adventurers—Fiction. | BISAC: JUVENILE
FICTION / Action & Adventure / General | JUVENILE FICTION /
Science & Technology | LCGFT: Action and adventure fiction.
Classification: LCC PZ7.K22485 Nh 2020 (print) | LCC PZ7.K22485
(ebook) | DDC 813.6 [Fic]—dc23
LC record available at https://lccn.loc.gov/2019025338
LC ebook record available at https://lccn.loc.gov/2019025339

10 9 8 7 6 5 4 3 2 1   20 21 22 23 24
Printed in the U.S.A.   23
First edition, February 2020
Book design by Keirsten Geise

Keep some room in your heart for the unimaginable.
—Mary Oliver

(This book is for every brave and curious soul
who does just that!)

Seven Years Ago

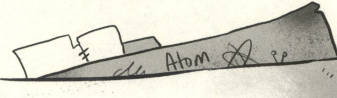

M—

I'm sorry that it's come to this.

Please know that if you ever change your mind, I will welcome you with open arms. We are in this together, whether you want to admit it or not. The world is depending on our technology to prosper. But if you're unwilling to do your part, I must proceed without you.

You know how much your friendship has meant to me over the years. But asking me to turn down billions of dollars and the chance for our invention to lead us into the future? I can't let you make this mistake. You and your family—even young Nikki, so bright already—have been so important in my life, and it's a joy to watch you all together. I regret that I won't get to see her grow up. And I very much regret that you won't either.

—Joe

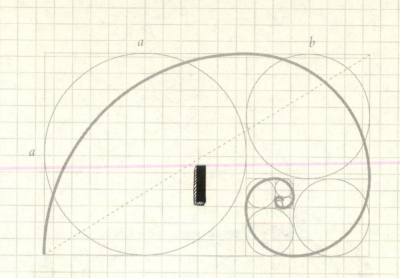

Okay, Tesla. You've got two minutes before your best friend dies. Get it together.

Unfortunately, my ferret wasn't cooperating.

"Pickles, I swear, if you sneak into my lab and pee on my equipment one more time, I'm going to personally build a rocket ship so I can send your little monkey butt to the moon." I dropped a folded paper towel onto the ground and swiped it through the wet puddle with the toe of my shoe. "Ugh!"

Honestly, how was I supposed to save my best friend *and* remain on the forefront of invention if my ferret wouldn't answer nature's call in her litter box like a normal pet?

unhelpful lab
partner

Pickles answered me by sniffing my foot, rolling onto her back, and nibbling at a newspaper clipping that had fallen from my desk.

"Hold it!" I demanded, reaching down to grab the tattered piece of paper before it got covered in her slobber. "That's not for you."

I blew the dust from the bold headline in my hands and set the article in the open drawer to my left with the others I'd pulled from the academy's archives. "You shouldn't eat newspaper," I scolded Pickles. "You're going to get a stomachache. Especially from something like this . . ." I cringed at the chaotic image in the story: Dad's laboratory, blown to pieces.

In response, Pickles lolled onto her belly and began chewing on the nub of my shoelace.

"Yeah, yeah," I said. "Keep on ignoring me. I see how it is." I leaned over and scooped her up, setting her on my desk. I used tweezers to grab one of the clear raised dots from my microscope slide and placed it on the tip of my finger just as my watch began to buzz.

"Shoot," I muttered. I was late. Mary wouldn't be happy.

"You see this?" I asked. Pickles snuffled the dot eagerly, licking her chops and preparing to eat it.

"Hey!" I scolded her. "It's not food." I yanked my hand away. "It's the *future*! Hold still. Remember what we talked about, okay? If this doesn't work, we're putting every-one here at risk. We're all relying on you. You've got to find her."

Pickles continued to watch me, blinking her choco-late brown eyes.

A word of warning to you: If you're ever in a life-or-death situation, don't trust your ferret to save the day.

At least, not until she's better trained.

I pulled her blue collar away from her fur and affixed the dot to it, sticky-side down. "Now go find Mary," I instructed. "Her life depends on it! Do you hear me?!" I smacked the table to show my urgency. "Go!"

Pickles seemed to understand, because she tore out the room like, well . . . like a ferret in search of food. You haven't seen speed until you've seen that.

I pressed a button on my watch and followed the ticking seconds, growing more nervous by the second. Only two minutes to go before the whole thing was a bust. I tried to distract myself by pacing, but every squeak of my sneakers on the marble floor reminded me of Mary. She was probably sitting on the very same floor right now, waiting for me and my undisciplined ferret to rescue her.

Sorry. Am I getting all life-and-death dramatic too early in the story here? I should probably introduce myself, especially if you haven't read any of these official government records before.

I'm Nikki Tesla, and there are a few things you should probably know about me before we continue. The first is that I'm a genius. I'm not saying that to impress you. I actually *am* a genius. In fact, I attend Genius Academy, a special school for kids like me with skills that tend to put us, or those around us, in danger. (They say danger, but I say *fun*, you know?)

My best friends are Mary Shelley (that's who my ferret, Pickles, is trying to save right now), Grace O'Malley, Charlotte Darwin, Adam Mozart, Leo da Vinci, and Bert Einstein. You probably haven't heard of them because Genius Academy is top secret. That's why the government will censor anything I say about where the school is located, what we get up to around here, or anything else they deem inappropriate.

Wanna see?

Genius Academy is located in ███████████.

Genius Academy is run by a super smart (but also oddly terrifying) woman named Martha ██████████.

The government spends over ██████ million dollars a year on our laboratory spaces, private jets, security, and ice cream truck.

See? I'm not allowed to tell you anything top secret. (For the record, that on-site ice cream truck is spectacular. You have to try the mint chip if you're ever in the area.)

But ever since the super-cool-but-admittedly-fairly-dangerous death ray I invented was stolen last month by a madman who almost used it to destroy the world for profit, I've decided to keep these records indefinitely. You know, just in case the government decides to blame me for any more destruction of property or global melt-downs. I think of them as insurance.

Sometimes I'll even get Leo to include some pictures for the sake of clarity. He's a pretty great artist, but don't tell him that or he'll be impossible to live with.

Thankfully, the days of risking my life and nearly destroying the world are far behind me. At least for now. That should bring you up to speed.

Oh, time's up.

My watch buzzed and I cursed out loud.

Exactly three seconds later, Mary's resigned voice interrupted my thoughts.

"And she's late," she muttered. "They're going to kill me."

Mary wasn't in the room with me—she was in my *ear.* Pickles had found her two seconds too late.

But it was working! I scrambled for my notes. "Mary! Mary, can you hear me?"

A brief commotion of rustles and squeaks erupted in my ear. I could envision Mary picking up my ferret and inspecting her. "Nik? Is that you? I can hear you, but where are you?!"

"Yes!" I exclaimed. "It's me! I'm in my lab. You see that little dot on Pickles's collar? It looks like big water drop."

"I see it!" she said. Pickles squeaked again. "I can hear you so clearly, it's almost like you're right here. How on earth did you do this?"

I squirmed, eager to test my technology. "Try pressing it like a button. Just once."

"*Okayyy.* But this thing better not blow up while it's on your poor ferret. Hold still, Pickles . . ."

Swiping the strands of messy hair from my forehead, I pulled an identical dot from my earlobe and stuck it to my desk. A faint crackle sounded, and instantly, Mary's face projected in front of me, suspended above my desk. If I'd done my job right, she would be seeing my face in front of her as well, projected over the dot on Pickles's collar.

"Whoa!" she said. "This is real time?! I can see you!"

I waved and moved around, bobbing left and right so Mary could get a good feel for the device. "Isn't it awesome? Auditory transmitters are easy to find, but ones this small are usually finicky and hard to conceal. Plus, mine has added visuals!"

"But you're *late*!" Mary said, sticking her bottom lip out in an exaggerated pout. "I'm going to die! What a world!" She threw her arm over her eyes and swooned.

I gripped the swatch of fabric from her shirt in my hands and shook my head. "I'm so sorry, Mary—I did everything I could!"

I slammed the drawer beside me shut before continuing, feeling a little guilty for my delay. I shouldn't have let those newspaper articles steal my focus. I decided to blame it on Pickles, who couldn't really offer her side of things. "Pickles wasn't paying attention at first, and she peed all over the lab floor, so I had to clean it up, and—"

"You cleaned it up?!" Mary widened her eyes. "My life was hanging in the balance, and you took time to clean up your ferret's *pee*? Nikki, how could you?!"

"You're right," I said. "And if this were a *real* life-or-death situation and not some dumb training simulation four doors down the hallway, I'd probably have cleaned up the mess after you'd died. Or at least moved a little faster." I shrugged.

And I would definitely not get distracted by researching seven-year-old news items.

She grinned. "Yeah, okay." A soda can cracked open with a fizzy gasp in the background. "I'll let you off the hook this time. But next time I'm about to die—even if it's in a training simulation—don't leave me hanging like that! This is a pretty cool invention though." She swiped her hand through the displayed image in front of her, muddling my view for a moment.

I beamed at my reflection in the mirrored tile of my lab. Pickles may have been late reaching her, but my little audio visual dots were working incredibly well. Was there anything better than an invention that could change everything?

"Thanks! I'm calling them GeckoDots. I modeled the nanoparticles on the base after gecko feet, so it can stick to any surface without adhesive. You can see whatever I see. Check this out." I stuck the GeckoDot to my forehead, turning my head to scan in all directions. Mary would be able to see my entire laboratory as I moved.

Mary propped her legs up onto a chair and took another sip of soda. "Amazing! Did you show the others yet? I bet Leo is going to *love* them!" She oriented the dot back to face her, and waggled her eyebrows at me.

"Shh!" I said, turning around to check that nobody was walking by my open laboratory door. Mary knew all too well what she was doing when she mentioned Leo like that. She was convinced I liked him. As in, *like*-liked.

"Speaking of visuals," Mary pivoted, "have you thought about what Martha said? I know you don't want us to bug you about it, but . . . if she thinks your dad could be alive, maybe it's worth finding out"—she hesitated—"more?" I could tell by her breezy tone of voice that she was trying to be super casual. But I was onto her tricks by now.

I bit back the angry rant about to come out of my mouth. "What does that have to do with visuals, huh? You said 'speaking of visuals' and then ask *that*?"

Mary grinned sheepishly. "I was hoping you'd overlook that. You've got to be a little curious about him."

"Nuh-uh," I said. "You know how I feel about it, Mary. I'm not curious at all."

I kept my eyes forward, refusing to even glance at my secret drawer of newspaper clippings. Mary was Genius Academy's resident writer, which meant she had an uncanny knack for reading minds. If she knew I'd been researching Dad's so-called death lately, I'd never hear the end of it.

"I know." She reached out and gave Pickles a gentle pet. Her face flickered once more before she continued. "Sorry for bringing it up. I'm only trying to help. It's not good for these things to fester. If he's alive, maybe it's a chance to find out what actually happened?"

Here's the thing about having a perceptive friend: It's a total feelings fest. They never let you carry on with your life when there are *feelings* to explore. Let's dig into those *feeeelings*, Nikki! Let's swim in them till our fingers get all wrinkly with emotion and regret!

Oy.

I don't *do* well with feelings, you know? Especially hey-remember-that-time-your-long-lost-criminal-father-apparently-came-back-from-the-dead-why-don't-you-want-to-meet-him-after-seven-years-apart feelings.

I mean, who in their right mind would want to open up that Pandora's box of emotion? Isn't it better to leave history where it belongs, far, far, *far* behind you? Why dig up things you can't change? Sure, I wanted to know the truth. But that didn't mean I wanted to *talk* about it.

Thankfully, another loud crackle sounded overhead, interrupting us. This time it was the intercom system in my lab. Every floor of Genius Academy was outfitted with an amazing sound system. Sometimes we used it to pump music through the halls as we worked. But it was also the easiest way for Martha to wrangle us together when trouble was afoot.

And I was learning that trouble was afoot rather often around here. It was basically *always* afoot. That was why we had to do life-or-death simulations so regularly, even if we sort of phoned them in from time to time.

Martha's voice bounced off the marble tiling of the hallway outside and drifted into my lab.

"Hello, everyone. Be advised that there is an unscheduled meeting in the Situation Room in exactly ten minutes. Please secure your projects, save your work, and make your way there as quickly as possible."

"Do you know what this is about?" I leaned over to the small fridge under my lab bench and pulled out a drink.

Mary shrugged and set Pickles back on the floor, sending the image dancing in front of me. "Not sure," she said. "See you there?"

I considered the possibilities behind an unscheduled meeting with Martha. As a lover of itineraries, protocols, and training modules, she wasn't exactly an unscheduled kind of person. She was more of a color-coded-day-planner-with-extra-stickers type. Had the earth tipped on its axis? Was someone out to steal the Declaration of Independence? Were man-eating tigers currently swarming Manhattan?

The thrill of the unknown made the skin on my arms and neck tingle with anticipation.

"Why stop the party now?" I smirked. "See you soon."

Good thing I was officially done getting into trouble. Right?

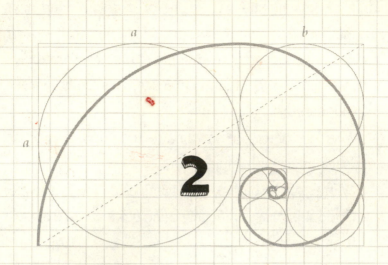

I yanked the thick drapes of the Situation Room half-closed, sending a block of shadow across the otherwise bright room.

"What are you doing?" Bert asked. "It's gorgeous outside! Let the sun in!" He rushed over to pull the drapes open again, only to have me wrench them out of his grasp.

"Charlie got a sunburn yesterday," I explained, rolling my eyes. I tucked the drape back into place so Charlie could have her shade. "Too much time outside." I tsked her, grinning at Bert.

"Oh, come on," he said. "Just because she's a cooked lobster, we all have to suffer? It's autumn and she's still crisping up like we're in the middle of July."

Having a bunch of geniuses under the same roof is kind of like wrangling kittens. Sometimes they will appease you and play together nicely. Sometimes they won't listen, and dart off the first chance they get, chasing whatever yarn ball of an idea they've got. And sometimes they like to complain, very *loudly*, about the injustices in the world.

Especially if those injustices relate to the other kittens . . . *er*, geniuses.

"Hey, it's not my fault," Charlie said. She tossed her blonde ponytail and stretched her bright red legs in front of her, wincing. "I'm practically see-through. I'm English, you know. Global warming is to blame! The sun is my mortal enemy! It haunts me day and night!" She scrunched her nose. "Well, mainly just day, I suppose."

Bert sighed. "Haven't you heard of sunscreen?"

"I *used* it! But I'd need SPF one *million* for these arms!" She flashed her beet red forearms and flipped them over to reveal silvery white skin on the undersides. Her voice took on a vampire-esque quality. "It *burnnns*!"

Martha watched in amusement as we all settled into our seats. As usual, everyone was doing their best to look attentive and awake. But also as usual: We were antsy. It was a gorgeous autumn day, and we wanted to goof around outside for once.

"Thank you all for being so prompt," she said. "I've got a lot to discuss with you today. But first . . . Ms. Tesla." She turned to me.

I instantly sat up a little straighter in my chair. Martha didn't usually address us individually until our mission was laid out, when she presented us with each of our assignments.

"Yes, Martha?" I forced myself to keep my attention on her and not the strip of sunlight on the floor, reminding me of the outside world. Bert was right. We *did* spend too much time inside, nerding around in our labs.

"I wanted to see if you'd given any thought to our previous discussion." She lifted her eyebrows and leaned back in her chair, her arms crossed over her chest. Classic Martha position. Her polished black leather shoes reflected disjointed squares of sunlight onto the ceiling.

My stomach tightened. Getting it once from Mary was bad enough. But now Martha, too? Did they have a "pester Nikki" quota they had to hit today? I decided to play dumb.

"Whatever do you mean? What previous discussion?" I batted my eyelashes at her, acting confused.

"The one about your father," she continued. She noticed me squirming and gave me a gentle smile. "We're

worried about you, Nikki. That's the only reason I'm mentioning this today. Your friends support you, and I think it's important you're open about the complicated feelings the news that he may very well be alive must have sparked. I want you to know that we're all here for you if you're finding this uncertain situation difficult." A pause. "*Especially* if you're finding it difficult."

I darted a look at Leo, who smiled at me in that easy-going but careful way he had. I could tell he wanted me to learn more about my dad. In fact, they *all* did. It was plain to see on their faces whenever the subject of my father came up. But it was easy for them to want that— their dads weren't criminals.

I gritted my teeth and got ready to give my usual response. I'd practiced it in the mirror a dozen times since our first conversation. I was getting pretty good at rattling it off without appearing angry.

So in one long breath, I said, "I'm *not* finding any of this difficult. I told you last month: I don't care about him. I know he might be alive. I know that evidence is indicating that he probably is. I've heard it all. But I am not interested in knowing any more. I don't want to see him. I don't want to speak to him. And I definitely don't want him to weasel his way into my life after everything he's done." I turned to the rest of the group, putting them on the spot. "Or do I need to remind you of what happened this summer? When one of his old colleagues stole my death ray? And tried to destroy the world? That ringin' a bell?"

Everyone stayed silent and stared at their feet. Clearly

this was as awkward for them as it was for me. I was glad for it: It meant they wouldn't push me on the subject any further.

Talking about my father like he was still a part of my life made me anxious. I meant everything I'd said. But while it was the truth, it wasn't the whole truth. I *was* terrified that he was alive. He obviously wasn't a good guy. No, he was a criminal who had tried to hurt people with his inventions. And his actions had made life practically impossible for my mother and me. It was tough on us when he'd died, but we were better off without him.

But the thing I refused to speak about? Even with Mary?

I didn't want to face the possibility that if he was alive, that meant he just . . . didn't want to see Mom and me again. If he had survived the explosion in his lab, why hadn't he come back to us? Why leave us alone for seven years, thinking he was dead? Seven years is a long time to pretend you don't have a family, even if you are a criminal. You only do something like that if you don't want your family anymore . . .

It was better to keep these thoughts locked up in a drawer in my laboratory, where questions and fears like this couldn't get to me.

I was grateful when Grace cut off my thoughts. "For what it's worth, Tesla, I agree with you."

I sat back in my chair, surprised. "You do?" A small blossom of hope grew inside me. Grace was our leader, and everyone always seemed to respect her choices. If I had her on my side, there was a chance we could sweep this whole father issue under the rug, where it belonged.

"Yep," she said. "You're right. You don't have any evidence that he should be back in your life. He broke the law and almost hurt a lot of people. And even after you thought he was dead, the people he was mixed up with did even worse stuff that *we* had to deal with. Seems pretty simple to me. So what if you're a little off because of it?"

"Yeah, thanks," I said. The meaning behind her words hit me a beat later. "Wait—what? What do you mean *off*? I'm not *off*, am I?"

I faced Martha first, then Leo. He caught Bert's eye, who almost imperceptibly nudged Leo with his shoulder. "Um . . ." Leo said.

"Um, what?" I demanded. "How am I off?!"

Bert lifted his hand, like he was apologizing for what he was about to say. "It's just that we can tell that your mind is a little distracted, that's all," he said, his eyes widening at the others, practically begging them to jump in.

But I didn't give them a chance. "Distracted?! We only wrapped up saving the world like a month ago, and I've been in my lab ever since, developing some pretty amazing surveillance technology that could totally change the way we protect others, *thankyouverymuch* . . ." My shoulders rose up to my earlobes as I spoke, and I wagged my finger at them with every word. I was officially turning into my mom.

"Your tech is great!" Charlie winced again as she leaned her elbows on her knees. "But two days ago you missed training because you forgot to set an alarm. And yesterday you left the door to the weapons hatch open."

"An accident," I muttered. "I thought Bert was going to close it behind him."

"What about all your late nights in the computer lab?" Bert asked gently. "You barely sleep. I know you say it's just research, but . . ."

My face went hot. "It *is* research!" I tried my best to sell my white lie. It was true I'd spent a lot of time printing those ancient newspaper articles about Dad's laboratory explosion, but they didn't need to know that. Had someone noticed my printouts?

Martha frowned. "And how did your simulation with Mary go this afternoon?"

I bit my tongue and forced my attention to a seam in the marble floor. "Pickles found her."

Mary cleared her throat but didn't correct me. I mean, it was sort of the truth. My ferret had found her eventually . . .

I squirmed in my seat as Martha scrutinized me.

"And you almost did a load of laundry with Pickles in the basket," Leo pointed out.

I darted him a look. "She had it coming, hiding from me like that!"

"We're simply getting a little worried about you. It's okay to be distracted. But we can tell there's something weighing on you," Martha said.

"What is this? Some kind of intervention?" Shame and guilt wrapped around me like a suffocating blanket. That my friends had noticed I was off my game was excruciatingly embarrassing. But we saved the *world* at Genius Academy—what if they thought I was so distracted, I couldn't do my job here? What if they worried that I would accidentally put people in harm's way? Could they kick me out?

"Is that what this is, Martha?" Tears pricked the back of my eyes, but I refused to blink and let them spill out. I swiped my sleeve angrily against my face and asked her again. "Tell me you didn't call this meeting because of me."

Martha gave me the tiniest smile. "Your friends requested that we discuss this again, Nikki."

The room seemed to shift around me, as everyone's shoulders tightened. Had they *all* requested it? Or one person in particular, and the rest went along with it? I was too ashamed to look them in the eyes to find out.

The truth settled over me and, suddenly, I could feel a familiar tightness settle in my chest, the invisible shield I built to protect myself and keep people at arm's length. These so-called *friends* ratted me out to Martha? How could they do that?

But I'd felt this way before, and my shield only hurt me at Genius Academy. And that realization made my anger dissipate as fast as it had appeared. It turned into something much softer, allowing me to see two very clear paths in front of me. Two possibilities. One: My friends were really were annoyed at me for being distracted. And two . . .

Mary read my mind. "It's because we care about you," she finished my thought.

I let my shoulders relax. Friends do worry about each other. "Okay," I said. "I get it. I'm sorry if I've been distracted. But I *just* found out that he might be alive. I need time to forget about him again. Or at least try to."

"Wait a second," Mary interjected. "Nikki, you're all

about equations. Your father is a huge variable in the equation of your life! How can you not want to know about what happened to him? Even if he is a bad man, don't you want any . . . any . . ." She trailed off.

"Closure," Charlie offered. "Knowing what happened to him would probably be a good thing, right?"

My throat tightened. "If he *is* alive, then he's not only a criminal who tried to blow up a bunch of people but also a jerk who abandoned his family. For *seven* years, guys. There are a million variables to this equation, but the final answer never changes. He left us. And now all these years later, Martha gets some random tip, and I'm supposed to jump at it? No, thanks." I sat forward in my chair so I could turn to look at each of them. "I know you guys are trying to help, okay? But if you want to help me, the best thing you can do is to let me deal with this Dad stuff myself, however I can."

Grace caught my eye and gave me the tiniest of nods. Solidarity. I had her on my side, at least. Mary, Leo, Charlie, and Bert avoided my gaze. Mo was always an enigma, but if I could count on him for anything, it was his silence.

"All right," Martha said, clearly satisfied. "Apologies for dredging up old wounds, Nikki. We'll move on to business."

"Great," I said, clapping my palms against my knees.

As she continued, I tried my best to focus on our next mission. But my friends' words had already begun to wind around me, squeezing the places where I felt most vulnerable.

I didn't need closure. I wasn't festering. Sure, maybe I was a little distracted. Who wouldn't be, right? But was I that off my game?

No matter what, I wanted the team to trust me. To know that I would never let them down, even if I was a little preoccupied with the news about my father. *They* were my family now, and my home.

I'd do anything to make sure they knew I wasn't flaking out on them.

Martha tapped her laptop, sending a projection onto the wall beside us. "The Galápagos," she began.

"What about it?" Bert asked.

Martha clicked the device in her hand and the screen changed, zooming into reveal a tiny island surrounded by beautiful blue water.

"Glad you asked, Bert." Her voice was measured and calm. "You're going."

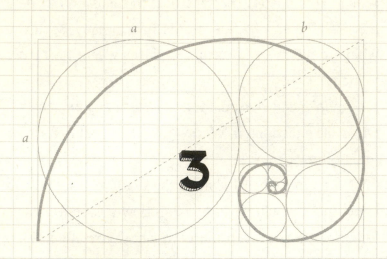

3

"Five hundred sixty-three miles west of continental Ecuador," she continued. "Home to tortoises, land iguanas, and even four endemic species of mocking-birds." Bright exotic birds smiled down at us from the screen.

Leo raised his hand. "Are we going on a *vacation*, Martha? It's been awhile, you know."

She tapped her laptop again, and the birds were replaced by a glass box sitting on top of a small pillar of rock. It was photographed in what appeared to be a shadowy, damp, mottled cave. Slices of bright light reflected off its shiny sides, making its contents impossible to see.

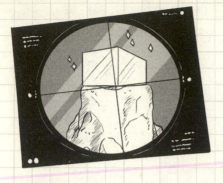

"You wish." Martha's eyes twinkled with mystery. "Our intelligence informs us that the Galápagos Islands are home to one of the most dangerous technologies known to man."

Have you ever heard that old wives' tale that every time you get a chill on the back of your neck, it's because a ghost is passing through you? Do you know the one I mean? I'm glad I don't believe in that nonsense, because at that exact moment, staring at that puzzling box, a chill zipped through me so fast, I actually shuddered. Something about that thing gave me the willies.

"Sign me up!" Charlie yelped. "We laugh in the face of danger!" She lifted her sunburned arm in a charge, then winced in pain. *"Ouch!"* She whimpered and rubbed her shoulder.

"You need some more aloe vera there, Danger?" Bert smirked at her.

The screen changed again. A tiny, lone island surrounded by crashing waves appeared before us. "I'm glad you're so eager, Charlotte. Though you may want to bring extra sunscreen for this one."

"Wait," Charlie said. "Are we *actually* going to the Galápagos?" She could barely keep herself planted on her chair.

"Indeed," Martha answered. "We've been hired from above to secure this technology."

Leo shot up his hand. "From above? What does that mean?"

Martha clicked her laptop again, and the screen went black. The mysterious box disappeared. "It means that up until recently, we didn't even know this technology existed. We do know that it has been kept secret, locked up in an unmarked cave. We're hoping that this is still the case, but recent intelligence tells us that this technology can be weaponized and that an unknown operative is looking to *sell* the technology to the highest bidder. As you know, the people who wish to buy dangerous weapons aren't always the good guys."

That got our attention. We exchanged excited glances, eager to hear more.

"Until we can confirm the technology is no longer for sale and will remain hidden away from the eyes of the world, it seems prudent for the safety of the country—and the *world*—to relocate it. And my lovely friends, your services were requested directly. I suggest you get packed as quickly as possible. Dress for the weather, of course. And bring any anti-nausea medications you think you might need."

Grace perked up. "Anti-nausea?" She grinned widely. "Does that mean what I think it means?"

Martha winked at her with just the tiniest flick of her eyelid. "There's only one way to explore the Galápagos, Ms. O'Malley."

Grace sucked in a breath and clapped her hands together. "By ship!"

"By ship," Martha agreed.

"Whoa." Bert stood up. "You never said anything about a *ship*. Can't we fly a plane and land it where we need to? Leo and Nikki handled that jet like professionals last time. Let's do that again!"

Grace laughed. "What's wrong, Bertie boy? Worried about a little seasickness? Can't hold down your Froot Loops?"

I bit my lip to keep from laughing. Bert was looking a little green already.

"Not everyone was born at *sea*, O'Malley!" he yelped.

"Sorry, Bert," Martha said. "You'll be taking a plane the majority of the way, of course. But to explore the Galápagos, and do so in a covert manner, we're going to

need a ship. We're lucky to have a certified sailor in our midst, wouldn't you say?" She gestured to Grace, who sat a little taller. Grace's face shone with pride.

I darted a look at Mary. All this sailor stuff was totally new information to me. *Was Grace really born at sea?* I asked her with my eyes.

Mary answered the question with a single nod.

Huh. I guess you do learn something new every day.

Even if you are a genius.

"Don't worry, buddy," Leo told Bert. "We'll bring some extra anti-barf tablets, just for you."

Bert didn't look pleased, but sat down in defeat. "So we're going to the Galápagos Islands to retrieve some super awful, extra dangerous technology and stash it away at a safe house? Am I missing anything?"

Martha clasped her hands together. "Just the part where you save the world from the evil people who plan to use this dangerous technology to harm others."

"Right," Grace said. "Can't forget that." She crossed her arms. "Sounds like every other Tuesday to me."

I chewed on this plan, and settled upon what was still picking away at my nerves. "Hold up," I said. "All this talk about secret technology. What exactly is it? What will we be securing?"

Martha hesitated before answering, tightening her mouth slightly. "It's a ring, Ms. Tesla. One with unknown capabilities." She pressed a button on her laptop, bringing up the image of the transparent box again. With a quick double tap on the screen, the image focused closer and the bright reflections of light faded away, revealing the very center of the box. Sitting atop three thin interwoven fingers of metal was the blurry but unmistakable image of a ring.

I exchanged glances with the team and held back a scoff. "A *ring*? Have we graduated to security detail for fancy department stores already?"

Martha sighed, but I could tell from the twinkle in her eyes that she wasn't annoyed at my comment.

"Finally, a mission I can get on board with!" Charlie clapped her hands together. "The Galápagos *and* a cute accessory. When do we leave?" She fluttered her eye-lashes and pretended to primp her hair. It wasn't like her at all, so her whole act made me giggle.

Martha closed her laptop. "This *cute* accessory must be secured as quickly as possible. Your flight leaves first thing tomorrow morning. Five a.m."

Bert rubbed his temple with one hand and sighed loudly. "*Always* with the five a.m. flights, Martha! Can't we save the world after sunrise just once?"

Martha didn't blink at his whining. "Morning might not come so early if you didn't spend half your nights playing video games in your laboratory, Mr. Einstein," she teased him. "I suggest you all get a good night's sleep. You'll need it."

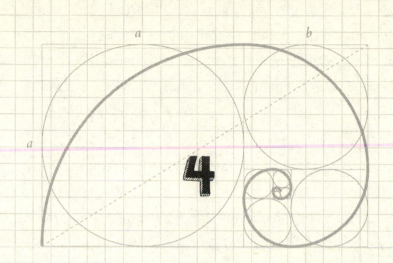

4

Grace held out the map at arm's length and shielded her eyes from the sun with her other hand.

You know those days where the sun is warm on your skin, but there's enough of a cool breeze to hide it, so you don't end up a sweaty mess? So far, stepping onto the Galápagos Islands was like that—a paradise of cool air, but with plenty of sunshine and wind to balance it out. Even the trees seemed to be showing off in their gorgeous climate, whispering and fluttering their leaves above our heads like they were happy to have visitors.

"Are we sure this map is up-to-date?" Grace made a face and twisted her hand left and right, trying to get the orientation correct. "It's supposed to be here."

As you probably guessed, Martha isn't usually wrong about details. She's one of those people with color-coded binders that can somehow account for every little element of a trip, like what donut shop has the best glazed donuts in every city in the world and which towns have police officers who are most likely to notice young kids out past their curfew. You know, useful stuff.

Her plan for our mission was straightforward: We were to fly to Guayaquil, Ecuador, where we would catch a smaller charter plane to Floreana, one of the tiny Galápagos islands nestled in the Pacific Ocean. From there, we were to take a diving boat to Corona del Diablo, a half-submerged volcanic crater that formed a ring of rocks jutting out of the water. There, Martha said, our ship would be waiting for us.

Easy peasy, lemon queasy, as barfing Bert would say.

But there was one thing she couldn't account for on this little journey: The ship was missing.

And yes, you're correct if you assume that we will literally *never* let Martha hear the end of this one.

Pickles clung to my shoulder and sniffed the salty air as a cloud of bubbles rising in the water made us all jump back on the jagged rocks. Leo's face, concealed in part by a set of swimming goggles and blue snorkel, appeared in the mess of foamy waves. As one of our strongest swimmers, he'd volunteered to do a little digging around (or, rather, *diving* around) to see if he could figure out why our ship was nowhere to be seen.

"Well?" Grace asked. She extended her hand to help Leo as he hauled himself out of the cold water.

He whipped off the goggles and shook his hair like a wet dog, showering us all with droplets of water. "That water is cold!" he said, rolling his shoulders to warm up. He flicked his hands at me, teasing Pickles with the droplets. Then Bert tossed him a red towel.

"Hey!" Charlie squeaked, hopping away from the drench zone. "Say it, don't spray it!"

He swiped his hand across his dripping face and shoved back his messy hair. The way the water was beading in his eyelashes made my stomach flutter, but I wasn't about to let anyone see that I'd noticed, so I went back to examining the surface of the water.

Oh, look. A fish.

"It's a good news–bad news situation," Leo said. He sucked in a huge breath, let it out again, and blinked quickly several times, as though to clear his vision.

"Bad news first," Grace said.

"The bad news is we do not have a ship," Leo confirmed.

"And the good news?" Charlie asked.

"The good news is . . . we . . . *did*? We're in the right place. But the ship isn't. Or, rather, it is. But it's not . . . available." He glanced down at the water.

Grace chewed her lip. "So it sank." As much as it

bummed me out that our ride was missing, Grace was probably more disappointed than any of us. She'd been so excited to sail a ship with us that she was even singing that pirate-inspired Disney song the night before on the plane.

Leo toweled his hair. "It sank all right. I can't make out exactly what happened, but judging by the barnacles on the bow, the ship's been down there for a while. Martha mentioned it was last used a few years ago, but I guess the satellites weren't tracking it as closely as they should have been."

"Great." Bert threw up his hands. Mo sidestepped away just in time to avoid getting smacked in the face. "So we're stranded here on ... Where are we again? Corona del Mario?"

Charlie snorted. "It's not a video game, dude."

"Diablo," Mary corrected. "Corona del Diablo. It means the devil's crown."

Bert stared at her, his mouth agape. "Well, I'm *so* glad to have you two around to inform me of my ignorance about the official nomenclature of the place in which we are now stranded. The Devil's Crown ..." he muttered, pacing the dock. "Of all the places to get lost. We'll need the devil's help getting out of here now."

Mo cracked a smile. "We're not lost. We know where we are."

"That's right," I said. I lifted Pickles from my neck and set her on the warm rocks to dry off a little. "If we know where we are, we know how to get to where we need to be. And that's over there." I pointed south, around the arc of the coastline.

Charlie clucked her tongue. "So what are our options? We can't exactly swim there. Or hitch a ride on one of those awesome marine iguanas I've seen paddling around." She grinned at Mo. "Though they are *fascinating*," she added. "Did you see the ones with the pink patches? They can dive up to a hundred feet and hold their breath for an hour, you know!"

"*Charlie*," Leo tried to drag her out of her zoological reverie. "Unless you plan on training one to get us there . . ."

"Right." She shook her head as if to clear it. "Not helpful, sorry. But we could construct a raft?" She looked to Grace for her input. "It wouldn't be that difficult. There's loads of material we can use back on the mainland of Floreana, and I could make some twine out of some of the vegetation. Sort of a Tarzan vibe, perhaps?"

"Or we could pretend we're stranded and flag down some tourists. Maybe we could ask them to take us where we need to be?" Mary suggested. You could always count on her for the most civilized, kindest ideas.

"And then we could take over their ship when they're not looking!" Charlie said. (She could always be counted on for the ideas that would land us in the most trouble.)

Leo shook his head, sending his wet hair into choppy angles against his forehead. "Too dangerous. If they get worried about us, they might call the cruise line authorities around here. A bunch of kids on their own? No adult in their right mind would be okay ushering us to a remote location totally unsupervised."

"What other choice do we have?" I asked. "If we don't get to the southern coast to pick up this so-called *most dangerous tech*"—I rolled my eyes at the phrase—"then our mission fails, and we're toast."

Beside me, Charlie rubbed her bright red shoulders. "*Burnt* toast," she added, wrapping a towel over the growing burn on her shoulders.

Grace eyed the horizon, and for a moment, I couldn't tell where she ended and the ocean began. She seemed to come alive next to the sea, like a houseplant that hasn't been watered in years. She began to hum the little rhythm she'd taught us, and a small note of mischief crossed her face.

"You can take the pirate out of the ocean. But you can never take the ocean out of the pirate." Her hand extended in front of her, pointing at the mottled image of something tall and gray looming in the water a few hundred yards away.

A ship.

It wasn't ours, of course. It probably belonged to some tourists. I was beginning to see an inkling of Grace's plan.

"There's our ride," she said.

I blinked into the distance. "Are you sure?" I questioned. "You want to steal a ship? Haven't we done enough of that lately? Stealing high-ticket modes of transportation? That's some bad karma." I was speaking, of course, of our last mission, when we'd stolen a jet plane to save the world. Stealing planes was so last month.

"*Borrow*," she said. "Tourists don't spend the day on their ships around here. They're off exploring, remember? We borrow it, take it to the southern coast. Boom, done. We can bring it back after."

"What about the tourists?" Mary said. "They'll be stuck on the island without food or water."

Grace shook her head. "Not if we leave them all their supplies. We've got enough for us. Plus, there are other tour groups and scientific studies going on around here, and they'll be easy to spot onshore."

Leo stretched his arms above his head and let out a loud yawn. "Well," he said, bending down to touch his toes to limber up after his dive, "I guess it's settled, then. Ready to steal a ship, me hearties? *Yo ho, yo ho* . . ." he began.

Grace grinned at him. "A pirate's life for me."

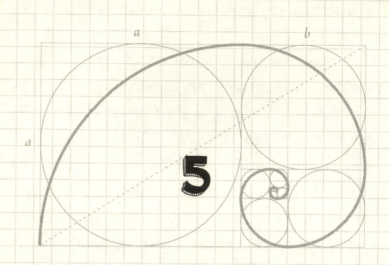

There are three ways to steal a ship. The first is to barrel in like a grizzly, flinging ropes around and making demands until you get the thing moving. The second option is to plan everything to the last detail and be very sneaky: Figure out who is going to keep watch, who's going to man the ship's wheel, who'll navigate, and who will distract anyone who needs distracting.

The third way to steal a ship is very simple: You wing it.

I don't recommend any of these options, to be honest, but desperate times and all. We decided to go with option three.

"Are you *sure* these boogie boards of yours are going to hold us up until we get to the ship?!" I gripped my homemade flotation device tightly against my chest and belly as the team kicked through the water. My neck craned to stay out of the salty ocean, but the waves were picking up fast, sending foamy spray straight up my nose. Charlie had gotten to be Tarzan after all, and fashioned us floating boards out of driftwood and vines from the island. We tied them together in a flying-V goose formation so we could stick side by side and stay afloat as we swam the short distance out to the ship.

At least, they were *supposed* to float. I was choking on an awful lot of salt water and fish poop for someone who was supposed to be leisurely gliding along.

"They'll last!" Charlie sputtered. She spit an arc of water at me through the air, narrowly missing my ear. She was second from the middle of our formation, next to Grace, who held the lead position. But when it came to these islands, Charlie was nobody's second banana. "I know every single thing about these islands! I'm not about to give you shoddy floaties that let you sink!"

"What's that fish always saying?" Bert's voice rose above the noise of the waves. "Just keep swimming! Come on, guys, I feel like I'm doing more than my fair share of the work here!"

"Your legs are longer!" Mary cried. "We're relying on you to do the lion's share!"

"I never signed on for that!" he bellowed back, but kept kicking hard.

"Hey!" Leo said, his breath coming out in choppy spurts. "Where does seaweed go to find a job?"

"Oh, no you don't!" said Bert. "No ocean puns, Leo!"

"The *kelp wanted* section!" Leo's gleeful laugh rose over the sound of the waves.

I laughed, nearly choking on another mouthful of

water. "How did the shark plead in the murder case?" I joined in. "Not gill-ty!"

We wailed with laughter as Bert groaned again. "If I wasn't about to barf because of the seasickness, that pun would have done it! You're killin' me, Tesla!"

"*Guys!*" Grace yelled. "We're almost there! No fighting on the floaties in the middle of the ocean, or I will turn this thing around and go back to shore, and you will never be allowed on another trip to recover dangerous technology again. Do you hear me?"

"*Yes, Graaaace,*" we all intoned in unison.

Fortunately, Grace was right. The ship that had been smaller in the distance was now almost directly on top of us. Only a couple of strokes more to go!

I hacked on another mouthful of salt water and tried to bargain with my racing heart. *Just a few more minutes! Don't fail me now! And then I promise you I will never force you to work like this again!*

We must have all been begging for the workout to be over, because we nearly crashed right into the side of the ship. It gleamed in the sunlight, with deep cherrywood beams forming the hull and a delicate white trim. A smattering of barnacles stuck to the sides, disappearing into the deep green water.

"Tesla!" Grace shouted, barely able to catch her breath. "Go for it!"

It was my job to scale the side of the ship and lower a rope for everyone. Gritting my teeth, I held tight to my mangled boogie board and reached around to my backpack, which I'd strapped as high as possible up onto my shoulders. Pickles nipped at my hand sharply as I dug around inside.

"I know, buddy." I moved quickly to avoid her teeth. "Sit tight in there. We're almost out of the water."

I could practically hear her sneer in annoyance as I found what I needed and latched the flap shut again before she could escape.

"These Gecko Gloves of yours had better work, Nikki!" Charlie said. "My legs are killing me!"

I shook the two adhesive gloves in the air, drying them off. "They'll work!" I said. I'd made them from the same material as my communication dots: a stick-to-any-surface invention that mimicked gecko feet. I hadn't expected to need them so quickly, but it sure beat trying our odds with duct tape or one of Charlie's homemade vine ladders.

I kicked again, positioning myself as close to the side of the ship as possible. Leo shimmied underneath my boogie board so he could help hoist me high enough out of the water to get a good connection with the ship's hull.

"Upsy-daisy!" he said, grabbing my calf and giving it a hard shove. The others joined in, connecting their hands to form a net beneath me and push me out of the water.

I stretched up as high as I possibly could. *Thwap!* The glove connected with the ship perfectly and, instantly, some of my weight shifted from Leo and the board below to my right arm.

Sweat poured from my forehead and dripped into my eyes, mingling with salt water. I shoved off from their hands again, and *thwapp*ed my left hand higher than the right. My arms now supported my full weight, and I hung suspended from the ship with both hands.

Don't try this at home!

Have you ever seen one of those little suction-cup stuffed animals? The ones that people stick up inside car windows? That should give you a pretty good idea of what I looked like. Only more waterlogged.

"Now!" I huffed, my shoulders screaming with the pain of holding myself up.

Below me, Mary and Charlie stripped off my shoes and slipped a second set of gloves onto my feet. You know, foot gloves, with toes and everything.

"Done!" Mary yelled. "Try climbing!"

I forced on my game face. *You can do this, Tesla. You are going to Spider-Man crawl your way up the side of this ship. It is the only way to ensure you do not become shark food. Now, GO.*

I pushed off my left foot with a grunt and began the climb.

"Shouldn't *Bert* be doing this?!" I barked down at the others, unable to control my panting. "Longer legs . . ." I took another difficult step, working against gravity the entire time as I crawled on all fours up the side of the hull. "Cover more . . ." Another step. "Distance!"

I didn't need to see Bert to know he was lifting his finger in protest. "Technically, it would take me greater energy to move the distance, because I'm much bigger! You could have taken your backpack off though. You're probably feeling that extra few pounds right now, huh?"

I snarled at him and kept up the work. My hands ached with exertion, and my butt was going to fall off any second. But I'd almost reached the deck of the ship, where I'd be able to haul myself up.

Just a few more inches . . . *There!*

I moaned something unintelligible as I positioned my elbows over the wood railing and gave one last kick with my feet. I tumbled onto the main deck in a heap of sogginess and exhaustion.

"Remind me never to do that again!" I wailed, thrashing my arms up over my face to shield from the too-bright sun above me. I shimmied my backpack off my shoulders and tugged at the flap, checking for Pickles. She was a little disheveled from all the water, but seemed to be as happy as I was to be on dry land. *Er . . .* dry ship.

"There you go, girl," I said. I let her out to scurry around the deck.

"Tesla!" Grace's voice boomed from below. "Lower the lifeline for us!"

"Hold on to your britches!" I wheezed. "I'm in the process of dying here!"

"Can you die a little faster?" Charlie joked. "I'm cold!"

"Yeah, and I'm hungry!" Bert added. "Aren't you

feeling a bit peckish, Leo? I bet you'd really go for some lunch, huh?"

"I could eat," Leo piped up from below.

I shook my head at their teasing. "It's all fun and games till you have to gecko your way up a ship," I muttered. "Okay, okay, I'm coming!"

I forced myself to stand on shaky legs and began scouring the railing for a ladder or rope that I could send over for the others. Bucket. Useless. Pad of paper. Ugh. Finally, I found what we needed.

"Guys!" I yelled over the side. "Swim over to the front of the ship by the bowsprit!" I pointed.

"What on earth is a bowsprit?" Bert called back.

"What, you didn't read the manual on this thing?!" I led them over to where a long post jutted out from the front of the ship. A pile of netting secured to the top would be perfect for them to climb.

"Heads up!" I yelled. I untied the mess of netting and let it fall.

I have to admit, watching Bert trying to navigate the shaky net was one of the funniest things I'd ever seen. He was like a dizzy spider trying to untangle himself from a web.

"You're all elbows and knees, Bert!" I giggled. "Put your back into it!"

When everyone was on board, Pickles scampered up to us again, slipping and sliding on the polished deck. The fresh ocean air brought out her playful side, and her eyes shone with excitement, almost as if to say, *What's next?!*

Mary leaned over to pick her up and let my ferret nestle into her shoulder and ear. "Good girl, Pickles," she said. "You were very brave. And I think we need to especially thank Nikki for all her hard work scaling this ship."

I bit back a smile and batted my lashes at Bert. "I'm *waiting.*"

He bowed low. "Nikola Tesla, you are by far the most accomplished user of gecko hands I've ever seen. Brava!"

I grinned smugly. "Thanks," I said. "I'm glad the hard part is over."

Grace snorted. "That's an optimistic outlook," she said. "You do realize we still need to sail this ship to the south and break into a highly secured secret cave, right?"

I frowned. "Sure, but first . . ." I gripped my growling stomach. "I have something to ask you."

"I know, I know. Lunch first, right?"

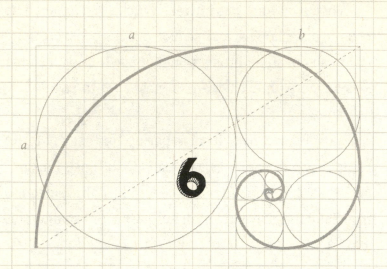

The domed cave loomed in front of us like a hungry mouth looking for a meal. After sailing with the wind for hours, taking some catnaps (and ferret naps), and stuffing our faces with protein bars from our packs, it had turned out to be a pretty great day. I mean, not including the whole stealing-a-ship thing. And my aching shoulders that would probably never forgive me for the horrible workout they'd had.

According to Martha's instructions, the secured vault containing the ring we were supposed to steal was inside the cave's mouth. The ocean floor sloped low right beside the rocks, so we navigated as close to the land as we dared.

"For a group of geniuses who are supposed to help people," Charlie began, "we do an awful lot of stealing." She examined the drawing of the vault that Leo had pieced together from some of Martha's notes. We had no idea how deep the path into the cave would lead, so we were packing extra supplies just in case.

"Do you think we could ever, like, *ask* very nicely to have whatever is inside a vault we're stealing from? It might be easier. Pretty please?" Charlie tossed her ponytail over her shoulder and pouted, sticking out her lower lip.

"Robin Hood stole all the time, and he was one of the good guys. Do you think *he* asked for an easier job when he was working?" Grace smirked at her.

"Everyone take a head lamp!" Leo said, opening his pack and wringing out some of the water from its straps. "I have no idea what to expect in there, but you can bet whatever we're facing, it's going to be in the dark. Grace is going to drop anchor right outside the cave, so we should be able to hop over to dry land without needing to swim. But . . . leap big, guys."

I took one of the head lamps he was offering and loosened the strap so it would fit around my forehead. I wasn't one to be concerned about fashion statements, but

I was glad that I wasn't the only one stuck wearing one of these silly-looking things. Plus, it kept slipping down over my eyebrows and onto the bridge of my nose as I turned my head.

functional and stylish!

"Nikki." Leo waved me over. "Here, I'll fix it."

I caught the faint trace of a smile on Mary's face as I stepped by her to get my head lamp sorted. My hands gripped into fists to cover up the fluttering in my stomach.

"Thanks," I said.

Leo bit his lip and reached up to my head lamp strap, carefully shifting some of my hair out from underneath. "No problem. These things can be a pain." His hands moved quickly, tightening the strap and then realigning the lamp toward the center of my forehead. The tiny dimple in his cheek quirked as he assessed his work. "Is that better? Shake your head yes."

I shook my head to test the strap. "Yes." My voice came out a little too high-pitched, but I was able to cover up my embarrassment with a cough. "Ocean air," I explained. "Must be allergies."

He grinned. "It does take some getting used to, doesn't it?"

Grace's voice made us both jump. "Is everyone ready? I want us to pair up this time, jumping on land two by two and then moving in a line so we can watch each other's backs. Charlie, you're with me. Mary and Bert, Tesla and Leo, you're all together. Mo, can you bring up the rear on your own?"

Mo grunted in agreement. (For him, that was saying a lot.)

Grace continued. "Keep your wits about you, and the *second* you notice something is off, stop. We'll handle it together as a team."

"Sorry, Pickles," I said. I knelt down to hand her an almond from my pocket. She inspected it, turning it carefully before digging in. "You're staying on the ship, okay? We'll be right back for you, I promise."

A thread of regret tugged inside of me. I'd almost lost Pickles on our last trip. Ever since then, I got anxious pangs in my chest when I had to leave her. What if we didn't return and she got stuck on this ship without any food or help? The thought of her alone in this foreign place was too much to bear . . .

A hand squeezed mine. It was Mary, reading my mind again. "She's a smart girl," Mary said. "She'll be all right, Nikki." Mary wiggled her fingers at Pickles, who had perched herself on a deck chair. At least *she* didn't look nervous. She appeared to be enjoying a nice vacation. All she needed was one of those drinks with a little pink umbrella sticking from the top.

Grace and Charlie were the first to leap off the ship and onto land, followed by Mary and Bert. The C-shaped platform curve of grassy land that led inside the cave was waiting for us.

"Ready, Nikki? Want to explore a potentially lethal cave full of hidden secrets and booby traps?" Leo asked. He held out his hand to me.

I swallowed down my nerves and reached out to grab it. "You had me at lethal."

We leaped across to the grassy outcrop in front of the cave. My foot slipped a little on impact, but Leo was there to yank me close and stop me from falling.

"Gotcha!" he said. His hands gripped my shoulders tightly, then released when he saw that I'd regained my footing.

We walked two by two toward the mouth of the cave, with Grace and Charlie leading the way. I relished the

warm sun on my arms for a few minutes longer, certain I'd miss it the moment we stepped inside.

And boy, was I right.

The cave was bigger than I'd expected. Brown tufts of parched grass clustered around the opening, and a few random bushes and rocks lined the sides. The rock face, gray and cracked, was warm against my palm. And there was a definite *vibe* in the air: This was not a place that was often visited. No footsteps or signs of human visitors around the entrance. A few minutes after our arrival, Grace, Charlie, and Leo had all taken extra time to search the entrance for traps or other security measures. But they all agreed. It looked like a normal cave.

Of course, I'd learned from experience that things weren't always what they seemed. We stepped forward cautiously, edging together as a group.

I'd love to say that the moment we descended into the darkness of the cave, we knew instantly that we were in the right place. But no traps were activated. No red lights began to flash. The only thing I noticed was how *dark* it had become. The sunlight from outside filtered away with every step, and soon the only light came from the beams of our head lamps, which shifted and sliced through the air with every jostling step, crossing over each other in a chaotic spiderweb of pollen- and dust-filled light.

Every few moments, Grace held up her hand, and we all stopped, sometimes with one of our feet still hovering above the crunchy, rocky ground. She would inspect the cave wall, then the path in front of her. And then, when she gave us the signal, we carried on. Moisture settled onto the back of my neck. A lone, annoying trace of spiderweb stuck to my forehead, suspended between my head lamp and my ear.

Deeper and deeper into the cave we went, each step taking us farther from the safety of our ship. Until, finally, a voice rang out, halting us in our tracks.

"Wait." It was Mary.

"What is it?" Grace whispered.

The beam from Mary's head lamp swiveled to the right, focusing a spotlight on the wall above our eye level.

"Do you see that?" Mary asked.

"Uh . . ." Bert said. "The cave wall? What about it?"

"It's not right," Mary said. "The marks and divots in the surface of the rock . . ."

A footstep crunched forward. It was Leo, taking a closer look. He held his hand a few inches from the side of the wall, like he was afraid it might burn him. His head lamp beam scanned the wall slowly.

"She's right!" he said. "It's not a natural surface at all. There's a *pattern* here."

I squinted at where his fingers were pointing to the small scratches and bumps along the surface of the damp gray rock.

"I see it!" I exclaimed. The pattern was hard to spot. But if you unfocused your eyes *juuust* enough, instead of a random smattering of dips and marks from wind or rain, you began to see a repeating pattern, like the cave wall had been stamped in some fake-rock factory.

The rest of the cave may have formed naturally over millennia without being touched.

But the section of wall that faced us? There was nothing natural about it.

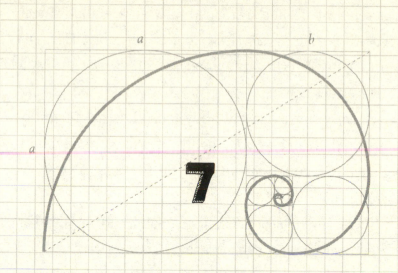

"This is some real Indiana Jones stuff," Bert whispered. "Anybody else got the feeling we're being watched?"

"This false wall must be the door to the vault." Leo stepped back from the rest of us and scanned the paneling with his head lamp again.

"If this is the door, how do we open it?" Charlie tapped her chin aimlessly.

"Should we start poking around?" I asked. I wasn't too thrilled about the idea of randomly knocking on a false wall in a hidden cave. What if we set off an alarm or released a cave troll or something? But what other choice did we have?

"That's our best plan," Grace said. The beam from her flashlight slid up and down the wall as she nodded in agreement. Then she stepped forward and took a deep breath, letting the air slowly out of her lungs. Her right arm extended, fingers curled gently to face the wall. "Here goes nothing."

Every muscle in my body tensed as her fingertips brushed the cave wall lightly. Gaining more confidence, Grace let her palm settle flat against the wet stone.

We all shifted on our toes, waiting for a noise, an electrical spark, or even worse . . . a booby trap.

When Grace turned to us, her expression was bright. *"Ta-da."* She faked a goofy bow.

Leo breathed a loud sigh of relief. "Nothing."

"Nope," Grace said. "At least nothing tactilely induced. Now we can work. Nikki, Leo, Mary, you take the left portion of the wall. The rest of us will do the right. Look for anything that gives us some indication of how to open this stupid door."

I strained to piece together the puzzle in front of me as we scoured every mark and divot on the wall's surface. The cave was very cold to the touch, and small rivulets of water trickled down from above us, forming almost invisible patterns at our feet. Mary and Leo ran their fingers over the wall and leaned as close as they could, with their noses only inches away.

While they tapped and explored, I tried to get inside the head of whoever had designed the vault in the first place.

If I wanted to hide something in a cave, how would *I* design the door? Would I have a password? Or a secret compartment? Would I press a button to reveal a hidden passage?

I stood back from the wall for a better perspective and tried to ignore the others. We were supposed to be retrieving what Martha called some of the most dangerous technology in the world, but to others, it would look like a simple ring. And what's more, it wasn't hidden in some big-city vault or advanced security system with guns or guards. Whoever had wanted to keep his secrets safe chose a cave on a remote tropical island to do the hiding.

Advanced technology in a simple space.

Big tech. Small cave.

What kind of a person would choose to do that?

Something obvious swirled around in my thoughts. Big yet small, it screamed at me, but I couldn't quite hear it. It was muted by my own uncertainty. No matter how much I forced myself to focus on the area in front of me, my attention kept tugging *down*.

Down to my feet.

Down to my toes.

Big tech. Small cave.

"Mary..." My voice was the only sound in the cave. Everyone was busy concentrating.

"Mm-hmm?" She didn't turn away from the wall to answer.

"Do you know of any stories with hidden vaults like this? Or secret spaces that reveal themselves?" I was grasping at straws, but if anyone could help me connect the shifting constellation of dots in my head, it would be Mary. I knew the others were listening, grateful for any inspiration.

Mary continued to run her hand over the surface she was examining as she spoke. "Oh, sure," she said. "There are lots of hidden vaults in books. One of the most famous is the 'Ali Baba and the Forty Thieves' story," she said.

"And how did they open the secret vault?"

Leo stood up and wiped his wet palms on his shorts. "They said the password," he answered. "Open sesame!"

Every set of hands froze in place as the others waited to see if Leo's password worked.

But this wasn't the desert or a tale in some ancient book.

"Worth a shot," he mumbled, and set back to work.

I tried to explain to Mary what I'd been thinking. "I was wondering about the kind of person who would store such a dangerous weapon here. All we know is that it looks like a ring, but it's supposed to be some huge advancement of science. And yet they chose to keep it in this rudimentary location without any security. Don't you find that a little . . ." I struggled for the right word.

"Sentimental," Mary said. "I don't know why someone would choose to hide something important to them in a place like this unless it's got some personal meaning for them."

"Maybe they like old-school methods?" Bert offered. "They could have read about some ancient passageway in a story, liked how mysterious it sounded, and wanted to store their technology in a place like that . . ."

"It does seem like something from a book, doesn't it?" Mary put her hands on her hips and rested for a moment. I could tell by the look on her face that she was circling the same puzzle I was. We were missing *something*, but I couldn't put my finger on what it was.

I tried to urge her forward. "I keep thinking we're looking in the wrong spot," I admitted. "This could be one big riddle—if we don't think properly, we'll miss the opening completely. This person clearly got some ideas from those old-fashioned, romantic stories about hiding treasure. Are there any other stories you can think of about secret passageways or places to hide things we don't want found?"

"Well . . ." Mary closed her eyes. Probably going through her bookshelves in her mind's eye. "The one that comes to mind is Alice."

A chill zipped through my body and out the tips of my toes. *Alice.*

And then a long-buried memory bubbled to the surface: sitting on my dad's lap while he read me the fanciful story of a white rabbit and a brave girl jumping down a magical portal in the ground. I hadn't thought of *Alice's Adventures in Wonderland* for years, but hearing Mary say the name made the sound of his voice ring in my ear as though he were sitting beside me.

"Magic is science we can't yet explain," he said. *"You only need to change your perspective to see it for the science it truly is."*

We'd gone on to read about Alice exploring a whole new world she had a hard time believing existed. At the time, I'd dismissed those stories because talking rabbits and secret passageways made no sense. Who needed magic when you had science, right? But something about Alice—about her journey down the rabbit hole to find the white rabbit—wouldn't let go of me.

After all, I needed to find a secret passageway right now.

I swallowed down the sharp memory and forced myself back to the present moment. Back to the cave wall. My fingertips tingled, still lingering on the old

memory I hadn't even realized I had. I tipped my head to the side, changing my perspective.

"You okay, Nikki?" Leo took a step closer to me, inspecting my face. He quirked his eyebrow.

"Absolutely," I said. I was grateful for the darkness, as I knew from the heat in my cheeks that my face was burning red. But there was no need to get into all the stuff about my dad right then. It didn't matter *how* I'd arrived at the answer. What mattered was I now had a hunch about the solution to our problem.

I knew why my attention kept tugging downward. *Alice* had been the key. My instincts were telling me to change my perspective.

Big tech.

Small cave.

Whoever hid his technology here appreciated the irony: having a massively important weapon hidden in a small, plain-looking cave. To get something *big*, we needed to think *small*.

But how do you think *small*? It's impossible to shrink your thoughts, isn't it? Maybe it wasn't thinking small that was the answer. Maybe we needed to *be* small like Alice, drinking the potion and shrinking down to enter the portal.

Only, in the real world, we didn't have to drink any potion. It was worth a shot, wasn't it?

"I think we're going to find the way in near our *feet*," I said. I don't know how I'd gotten to the solution, but I *knew* I was right.

The others faced me, confusion in their shining, flashlight-reflected eyes.

"Feet?" Grace asked. "Why? We should be inspecting the whole wall."

I didn't want to admit that I'd gotten the idea from something my dad had said to me all those years ago. Thankfully, Mary came to my aid.

"I think Nikki's right," she said. "We've got too much area to cover. Whoever owns this tech hid it here. That shows he has a flair for the dramatic. Nikki's idea will narrow our focus, which can only help us. And if she's wrong, we can still look elsewhere."

I threw her a grateful glance.

"Good enough for me," Grace said. "Concentrate on the bottom of the wall, everyone."

We all dropped to our knees and began inspecting the very bottom of the cave wall, where dust and pebbles sat in tiny piles against it. Using our hands to sweep them away, we were able to see portions of the wall that had been hidden. We got down to an ant's perspective, and pored over every indent.

"I've got it!" Mo said. He spoke up so rarely that the sound of his excited voice seemed almost foreign.

"What is it?" Leo skidded over beside him. "Did you find a button? Or a secret lever?"

We all shuffled over to where Mo lay on his stomach. He held a small magnifying glass in his hand, which was focused directly above a small pile of pebbles by his fingertips.

"Nope," Mo said. He handed the magnifier to Grace and pointed. I was close enough to see what he had found.

Not a button or a lever.

It was a series of letters and numbers, each barely bigger than my pinkie fingernail. They were etched along the bottom of the wall and had been hidden by rocks and dirt only a few moments earlier. Grace sat back on her heels and used her fingertip to brush away the remaining dirt, revealing the letters and numbers in full relief.

90 68 53 G1 T8 10 M92 16 T16 15 EA 19

"It's a code," I said. "And if we want into this vault, we need to crack it."

90 68 53 G1 T8 10 M92 16 T16 15 EA 19

I wish I could say we all sat down and started brain-storming happily, coming up with the answer at our leisure.

But unfortunately, that's when the cave began to shake.

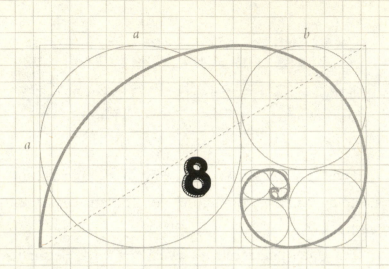

8

At first, it was hard to place the eerie, deep groaning sound emitting from the walls of the cave. It was almost mechanical, like twisting or grinding metal. Was an earthquake or volcano thundering under the ground? No. The noise was much sharper.

And much *closer.*

"Gears!" I shouted. I pressed a hand to the wall to feel for vibrations. Something was shifting and turning beneath my fingertips. "They're in the wall!"

Leo beat me to my next thought. "We've got to get out of here!" he yelled to the team.

"Go!"

We stumbled to our feet and hightailed it for the cave entrance. The sound of the moaning gears inside

the wall grew louder with every step, melding with the frantic pace of my own panting. My lungs burned with exertion and my breath was as loud as my feet on the dirt pathway as I raced to keep up with the others. Floating dust motes began to dance in front of us as we got closer and closer to the light. We weren't far—the sun was a beacon, guiding the way.

But something was wrong. The bands of bright sunlight were growing smaller and narrower as we pushed forward. We should have been running into *more* light as we exited the cave, not less.

"Not good, not good," Mo panted beside me. His arms swung madly as he ran.

We must have gone deeper into the cave than I realized. Finally, a bright pinprick appeared in front of us.

The entrance to the cave! But the wide mouth we'd come in through had shrunk to half its original height, and it was located much *lower.*

"What the devil is going on?!" Charlie screeched.

"It's the gears!" Leo said. "We must have activated them somehow when we touched the code! This cave has a door, and it's *closing!*"

He was right. The cave's entrance was slowly sliding shut, dropping from the ten-foot ceiling all the way down to the ground like some sort of ancient garage door.

The hole was growing smaller with every pounding footstep. Calculations whizzed through my mind. Could we make the impossible happen? I quickly considered the angles of the descent, how many of us there were, and the sheer speed at which the door was dropping. The truth was obvious . . .

We weren't going to make it.

"Slide!" Charlie yelled. "We can't get trapped in here!"

I squeezed my eyes shut as I pummeled forward, begging my body to do as it was told. If even one of us targeted our slide wrong, we would be crushed under the weight of the door. When I opened them again, I was terrified to see that the rock door shifted closer to the floor. How could nobody see that this was a terrible idea?!

"STOP!" Grace sprinted ahead like she had activated some turbo-speed button on her legs. She reached the door before us and held out her arms, blocking our path.

"What are you doing?!" Bert yelled as he skidded to a stop. The rest of us crashed into him, tripping over our own feet and falling to the ground. Eventually, we stopped as Grace had demanded and sank to a pile of panting mouths and twitching limbs.

Grace bent at the waist and let her hands rest on her knees as she caught her breath. Behind her, the door continued its crawl to the floor. Six inches left. Five. Four . . .

Seconds later, the door thudded shut and we were completely sealed in.

Silence and dust settled as the reality of what had happened sunk in.

"There was no way we all were going to make it out," Grace said. She shook her head fiercely and the light from her head lamp shot swishy beams through the damp air. "Not a chance. It's all for one, remember? We don't leave anyone behind." She wiped her sweaty face with the back of her hand. "And so, we *all* have to stay."

I rubbed the sweat and dust from my eyes and let my shoulders sink with relief. Frankly, I was pretty darn happy that none of us had been crushed to death under a massive rock door.

But that meant . . .

"We're trapped in here," Charlie said. She gripped her arms tightly and the whites of her eyes shone brightly as she rolled them to the ceiling, inspecting the space.

"Not true," Leo said. He patted Charlie's shoulder with one hand. "We can't get out this way, but we've still got the code. The code will lead us to the technology we're supposed to steal *and* it will get us out of here. I'm sure of it. Don't worry, Charlie, we won't be stuck here forever."

She smiled weakly. "Promise? Charlotte Darwin won't find her end in the Galápagos?"

"Duh," he said. "You've got much more to accomplish back home. We're seven geniuses. I think we can figure out one measly little code."

It's easy to feel resigned to your fate when you know you only have one choice. We trekked back to the wall where we'd discovered the code and tried to focus, ignoring the fact that if we didn't figure out what it meant, we would all be stuck in here forever.

Martha would have no way to find us. And Pickles would be on her own again, this time on an empty ship.

My heart clenched.

"Does someone have a pencil and paper?" I asked, desperate to get to work. To feel some kind of control in this claustrophobic situation. I couldn't shake the feeling that we were in an enormous coffin. At least, that's what it would be if we didn't make it out of here.

Would our remains ever be found?

"Here." Mary snapped me out of my morbid thoughts. She handed me a small pad of paper and a worn pencil. "Nikki, you came up with the idea of where to look for the code itself. I think you should take the lead on this."

I looked to Grace for her approval.

"Agreed," she said. "You seem to have a knack for this. Let's brainstorm."

I sat cross-legged on the floor by the code, and everyone settled around me in a circle. I transcribed the letters and numbers carefully, then made a duplicate for everyone so they had their own paper to examine.

"The highest number is 92," I began. "The lowest is 1. Anyone have any ideas?"

Leo held up his paper. "I think the code might be a sequence of words. Each number could represent a letter in the cipher," he said. "But it's interesting that we've already got *some* letters here to work from." He listed on his fingers. "G, T, M, T, E, and A."

Charlie scratched the letters into the dust by her feet, fiddling with the different orders. "What does that mean? Why wouldn't every letter be assigned to a different number?"

"Maybe the cipher doesn't have a way of including certain letters?"

Bert frowned. "What good would it be, then?"

"It makes things more difficult," Grace huffed.

"In many cases, ciphers use a key word." Mary scribbled something on her piece of paper. "So in a way, this is easier. The code tells us that whatever the key is, it *isn't* a word. At least not one in the traditional sense."

"So what contains letters, but isn't a word?" Bert scratched his head.

"That sounds like a riddle that Gollum would ask us," Mary said. She clasped her hands together and squeezed for a moment, turning her knuckles white.

"Huh?" Charlie asked.

"In *The Hobbit*," Mary clarified. "Remember? Gollum kept asking Bilbo a bunch of riddles, and he had to get them right if he wanted to escape." She recited the riddle: "Voiceless it cries, wingless flutters, toothless bites, mouthless mutters."

We all stared at her, waiting for the answer.

"The wind," she said, lifting her eyebrows. Even

talking about books seemed to lighten her mood. "It can cry, flutter, bite, and mutter, you know?"

"I always liked that first *Lord of the Rings* better," Mo said. "Legolas is the man."

Mary sighed dreamily. "No argument there."

"We *are* a kind of fellowship, I guess," Charlie sniffed. "Though I'm very glad there's no Gollum in this situation. I don't think I could handle a half-naked little weirdo running around in here with us, rambling about taters or *precious* rings."

"No Gollum that we *know* of," Bert pointed out.

"Fellowship!" Grace clapped her hands to get our attention. "Focus, yeah? What has letters but isn't a word!"

"Right," Bert said, getting back to business. "It must be something where the letters are ordered, since we're trying to match each number to a letter to make any sense."

"Maybe a flight schedule?" Charlie said. "They pair letters with numbers and times."

We began compiling every instance we could think of where letters were paired with numbers. Flight schedules, famous street names, even grocery checkout codes for produce.

After an hour of fiddling, Leo tossed his paper aside

in frustration. The air inside the cave was starting to make my skin clammy and itchy, like I was sitting in a tepid bowl of soup.

"None of these are working," Leo said. He was stating the obvious, but I was grateful for a chance to stop re-arranging numbers in my head.

We'd managed to find the code itself by thinking small. Maybe we could solve it by doing the same? I don't know why, but it was almost like the walls, with their tiny code, were talking to me.

I just couldn't hear what they were trying to say.

I tried out my theory on the others. "Guys, what if the answer to the code can be found the same way we found the code itself? By thinking small in this huge space. Is there something there? What's small in size but can also be all-encompassing like this cave?" Curiosity and fear mingled together in my chest and hovered over my heart. I knew I was onto something but had no clue what it was. Or maybe I was just dehydrated and would soon be hallucinating about Gollum stealing the apple in my backpack.

"Thinking small?" asked Leo. "What do you mean?"

"Yeah, smaller than *what*?" Bert interjected. "This is madness! Smaller than letters? Smaller than numbers? Negative integers? There are too many choices!"

I looked blankly at Leo, but my thoughts were far, far away, desperately trying to untangle themselves.

Magic is science we can't yet explain.

"I don't know!" I yelled, frustrated at this whole puzzle. "All I know is that we found this dumb code by thinking and *being* small, so I thought maybe if we did the same—" I tore up my paper, chucking the pieces in the air. One settled onto the front of my chest. I brushed it aside angrily.

"I've got it!" Leo turned to face me. "What about atoms?"

Bert lit up like he'd just solved the theory of relativity. "That's it!" he exclaimed. He began scribbling on his paper and used Grace's for reference for the original code. "Atoms! *Atomic numbers*, you guys!"

"The periodic table of the elements!" I said. *"Yes!"*

"That has to be it!" Leo said. "Ordered numbers that correspond with certain letters. And it explains why some letters are already included. G, T, M, E, and A aren't used as atomic symbols! So what does the code say?"

"I'm working on it!" Bert snapped. "90 is thorium, and 68 is erbium, so our first word is *the*. That's a good sign! That leaves us with an R, and with 53 as the atomic number for iodine, that means the next is an *I*. Hydrogen is the number 1, which means our next word is *right*, and atomic numbers 8 and 10 are oxygen and neon, respectively, so that's *one*..."

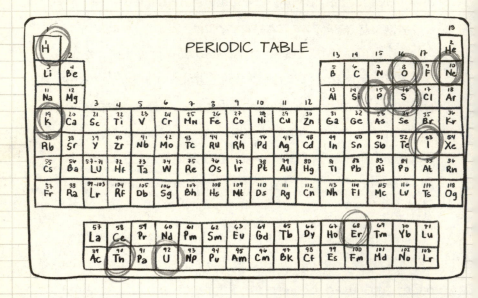

We all watched as he decoded the rest of the message. My heart, which had been thumping madly in my chest a few minutes before, seemed to limp to a halt as the letters revealed themselves on the paper. I don't know what I was expecting. Maybe that the code would turn out to be a sequence of words we could read aloud, making the vault magically open? A sentimental password or name?

But instead, the solution seemed to be only one stage of the riddle. It wasn't a phrase to read out loud, it was an instruction. Or maybe, a warning.

The right one must speak.

"What do you think it means?" Grace whispered, suddenly aware of the message behind the code. "Who is the right one to speak?"

We all exchanged glances, but nobody knew where to begin answering that question.

"And more importantly"—Charlie shuddered—"what happens if the *wrong* one speaks?"

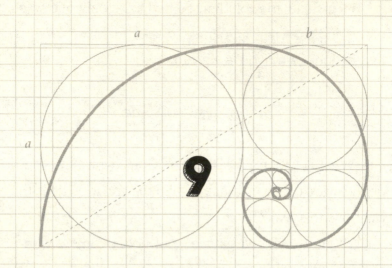

There are some moments in your life where you have to sit back and wonder, *How on earth did I get here?* This was one of those moments. Just a few months ago, I was stuck working out of a makeshift laboratory at home with my mom. My best (and only) friend was Pickles, and I spent my days inventing things that sometimes (okay, *usually*) blew up portions of the house.

Why couldn't I get those days out of my head now? A sad, aching pull in my chest tugged me back to a time when it was just Mom and me, with two place settings at the table. Bert was right; I *did* feel like I was being watched.

But not by security cameras.

I felt like my past was sneaking up on me, stalking me like a stealthy predator on silent paws. But, of course, that made no sense. I knew the others had my back—so what was I afraid of?

Why couldn't I shake the clammy chill on the back of my neck in this awful cave? I could only hope that whatever was inside this vault was worth it.

Grace must have sensed our frustration and fear, because she forced herself to her feet and stood tall. "We're almost there." She rubbed her hands together, as though she was trying to light a fire under us. "The right person must speak. Maybe it's simple: The person *on* the right must speak."

"What right though?" Charlie asked. "Standing on the right facing the wall? That would be Leo. Or from the vault's perspective, the person on the right?"

"Who would appear to be on the left," Bert clarified. "Which would be me."

"Or it could mean the right person, like the correct person. Or the person that is meant to do it in the first place. Or *destined* to do it." There was an edge to Mary's voice that sent a shiver across my skin.

"Plus," Leo added, "we don't exactly know what the right person is supposed to say. Are they supposed to speak and say anything? Or can they order a cheeseburger and the door will still open? We've all been talking this whole time, anyway. Who's to know?"

Grace threw up her hands in frustration. I couldn't blame her. It was way too easy to get lost in what-ifs. "Let's just each try asking the cave to open for us," she decided. "This day is weird enough, what's a little talking to a wall while we're at it?"

One at a time, we spoke aloud, trying to convince the vault to open. Mary asked politely. Charlie begged. Grace asserted very clearly. Even Mo hummed a little rhyme to convince it to open up.

"This is getting ridiculous. Talking to a cave?" I fumed, when it was my turn. Turning to face the wall, I couldn't stop my voice from rising in annoyance.

"Hey!" I screamed at the wall and pounded my fists against its hard wet surface. "Let us in already! *Please!*"

The one good thing about yelling in a cave? You get a fantastic echo. And that echo gives you the teensiest bit of satisfaction when you're annoyed, so you get to hear your anger bounce back at you and reverberate in your ears dozens of times.

The bad thing? It doesn't do a lick of good. In the end, you're still stuck in a cave.

"Nikki." Leo's voice was calm. "Why don't you sit down and relax for a minute. We'll figure this out."

There were a few mumbles of agreement, but I didn't have time to answer.

Why? Because the wall in front of us began to shift.

Leaping back, we watched in shock as the thick slab of rock grumbled and groaned. Tiny pebbles and dust fragments tumbled to our feet. A faint streak of gold light poured out from a slit that appeared in the wall before us. It grew wider and wider, like a cat's vertical pupil, yawning open in the dark.

"Get back!" Grace instructed.

"Did yelling actually work?" Bert said, scrambling back to steer clear of the skittering pebbles at his feet. A low whistle escaped his lips. "I guess we know who the right person was," he said.

I ignored their stares and gawked at the room appearing in front of us. Its walls were the same mottled gray as the cave itself, with small rivers of water dripping down the sides. The space was very cramped and lit from within.

I shielded my eyes against the bright spotlight that was trained on a single gray pillar in the middle of the room.

"This *is* some Indiana Jones stuff," Bert breathed in awe.

On the pillar sat a glass box, exactly like the one from Martha's notes. There were no red lasers protecting it, or weird marks on the floor, or even basic "Do Not Touch" warning signs.

It was just sitting there, waiting for us to pick it up.

As my vision adjusted to the bright spotlight, the contents of the box became clear. Something silver and round sat perched atop the three bands that swirled together in a nest of metal, glinting and winking at us in the light. Sparkling like iridescent fish scales, or vibrant metal.

Martha was right.

It was a ring.

"Who do you think should grab it?" Bert ventured. Nobody moved.

I bit my tongue. I knew what answer was coming. But that didn't make it any easier. For some reason, this cave seemed made for me, from the *Alice in Wonderland* perspective to the voice-activated door. Even the tiny box sitting on the pillar right now practically called out to me.

Was I the right person?

And if so, why?

I stepped forward into the light. My skin prickled with that familiar combination of fear and curiosity that I'd felt ever since we'd stepped foot in this damp hideaway. I'd never seen this object before. But it made a bizarre sort of sense that it had to be me to pick up that ring.

I didn't want to hesitate. Didn't want to think about the booby traps that taking the ring off the pillar could activate, or worry what might happen next. We had to neutralize this dangerous weapon and get out of here. Back to Pickles. Back to safety. And that meant I had to act.

Was the electric spotlight emitting that weird, distant hum?

Or was it the ring itself?

I grabbed the box from the pillar. "I'd say we're about to find out."

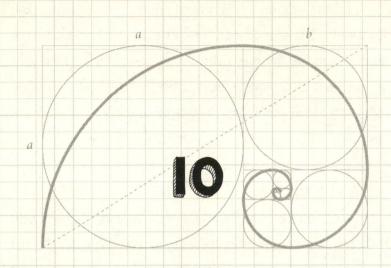

You know what feels good after being trapped in a sweltering cave and solving ridiculous codes all to grab some tiny, sparkly, supposedly dangerous ring?

A *shower.*

You know what sucks about that shower?

Waiting for *six* other people to go first, because the stupid ship you're on has only one bathroom.

That's right. My name is Nikki Tesla, and I'm a sweaty, stinky, ring-stealing mess. And I drew the shortest straw in our shower lottery.

After we'd finally made our way into the vault and stolen the ring, things went pretty much according to plan. No alarms went off. The door to the cave mysteriously cranked itself open again. And no Gollums erupted from the walls to chase us to our dooms. But we did have one surprise when we finally made it back to our ship, panting and whimpering with exhaustion and sweat: For the first time since I'd known her, Grace offered to cook dinner. She never let on at the Academy, but it turns out that Grace is a whiz in the kitchen, especially if that kitchen is located on a ship. Within minutes, the delicious smell of sautéing onions and garlic and the tinkering sounds of a meal being prepped drifted through the cool, salt-filled air.

"I know," I mumbled to Pickles as she nestled into my shoulder on the cot we were sharing in the ship's barracks. "I missed you, too." She used the back of my head as a scratching post but kept the pressure playful and gentle. Ever since I'd nearly lost her, she had been as sappy as a maple tree in March.

"But it was worth it," I continued sarcastically. I groaned as I stood up, reaching for the small transparent box. "Look what we found."

Pickles sniffed at the box, enchanted by the sparkling ring inside, while I inspected the plastic, lifting and turning it to examine it from all angles. The ring itself was beautiful, sure. Silver, with wide clear gemstones of some kind set deep within its band. Tiny flakes of silver overlapped the entire circle, giving it a distinct, scale-like appearance. It almost looked like it would start moving

on its own at any second. Iridescent and glittering, it seemed to capture and reflect every bit of light that hit it.

But we weren't here to save the world from something beautiful. Martha had been told that this ring was *dangerous*. Some of the most treacherous tech known to man.

We'd almost died for this thing.

I growled and set the box down again. The waves surrounding our ship sounded like a giant heaving deep inhales and exhales in the water. Slowly, my own breathing began to mimic the sound. Dropping my chin to my chest, I stretched the back of my neck and tried to think clearly.

It obviously wasn't just a ring.

Martha would never be wrong about something like this. It was pretty clever to hide amazing tech in such a small, simple object. But it wasn't enough to know *that* it dangerous. I wanted to know *how*. Chewing my lip, I checked over my shoulder.

Bert and Mo were helping Grace with dinner prep. Charlie was hiding out from the sun under a makeshift umbrella on deck while Leo dug through online data-bases for any information about the ring and whoever was hoping to sell it. Mary was up next in the shower. Everyone was occupied.

Have you ever done something you *knew* was a bad idea? But you couldn't stop yourself because you know you'd always wonder what would have happened?

Of course you have, and that's why you understand why I had to open that box.

The ring was lighter than I expected. In the box, it looked like some sort of metal alloy. But holding it in my hand? It was clear that the material was different than any-thing I'd ever seen before. It was almost pliable, weighing no more than a few grams, and eerily warm to the touch—not the way any metal should feel. It was also larger than I thought, like it was meant to fit a man's finger.

I brought the ring to my nose and gave it a quick sniff. Traces of cold rain and the smell of damp earth met my nostrils. Definitely a material I wasn't familiar with.

That's when the buzzing started. No, buzzing isn't the right word.

Humming.

The ring got warmer in my hand. It wasn't flashing or beeping like a watch or alarm clock. It was expanding and contracting ever so slightly, almost like it was breathing.

Like it was *waking up*.

I'll admit it right here. Let the record show that I, Nikola Tesla, know that what I did next was totally, completely, and unforgivably wrong. I have no excuse and deserve every ounce of trouble thrown my way for the rest of my life. I'm the one to blame for every terrible thing that was to come.

But sometimes, the only way to get real answers is to take a risk. To stay curious no matter how much people tell you otherwise.

Before I could talk myself out of it, I slipped the ring onto my finger.

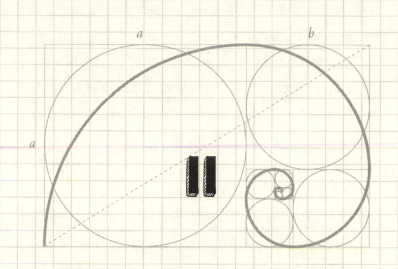

What happened next was nothing I could have ever expected.

That is, *nothing* happened.

I sat there, with the too-big ring on my pointer finger. It was still warm to the touch, and a light, eerie hum kept emanating from it. But diddly-squat was happening. No fireworks. No blinking lights. No Iron Man moment.

Nada.

I frowned. I mean, I don't know what I was hoping for, but for something known for being the "most dangerous technology in the world," I thought I'd get a slightly bigger display than just a faint hum. Pickles didn't seem to care. She stretched her legs and scurried up to me. I could tell by the way she was eagerly sniffing my hands that she was hungry.

"Hey, not so fast, you little maniac." I gently shoved her away so I could squirm over on the side of my butt to reach inside my pocket. If you have a ferret, it's crucial to pack snacks in your pockets to avoid ferret tantrums. Pulling out a shelled peanut, I set it on the ground and gave it a little flick with my finger.

But Pickles barely blinked at the treat. Instead, she crouched down on her belly and stuck her rear in the air. She stared at me, like a dog waiting for a ball to be thrown.

"Earth to Pickles." I poked her gently. "You know you're hungry, so go get it." I reached over and grabbed the peanut again, this time placing it in my palm for her.

She snuffled the peanut, then began nipping at my hand. She wasn't biting hard—just enough to pinch, a playful kind of biting she used to do as a kit. "What is *up* with you, weirdo?" I grabbed her in one hand and held her to my face, peering inquisitively into her eyes.

Unfortunately, she was getting more annoyed by the second, twisting and scratching at my hand. Her tiny claws left red marks on my wrist, and her squeaking got so frantic, I had to set her down.

The minute her toes touched the floor, she leaped at me again, this time making a beeline for my hand.

"Hey!" I shouted. "What is wrong with you?!" I lifted my arm out of the way just in time to avoid her teeth. I think you know me enough by now to realize that I would *never* hurt Pickles. Not even a tiny shove or nudge that could harm her. So my heart started pounding against my throat when she cowered in front of me.

Well, she wasn't cowering from *me* exactly. She was fixated on my hand.

I swallowed hard and tested out the movement, lifting my hand to the left. She scampered on her feet and shifted left, keeping herself directly underneath my hand.

"*Hoo-kay,*" I muttered. "So you don't like this thing. It's okay, bud."

I moved my hand slowly over her head, this time to the right. Her neck swiveled to follow, and her tiny feet shifted beneath her. No matter what I did, she angled herself to face the ring. Maybe along with the humming, it was emitting a frequency that scared certain animals? Perhaps she heard something that I couldn't, like a dog whistle.

"It's all right, girl," I said. I used my right hand to scoop her up and give her a cuddle. "I promise, whatever this thing is"—I held my other hand up for her inspection—"I don't know how to use it. In my hands, it's a glorified fashion statement."

Seeing me relaxed seemed to help her calm down. She hopped out of my hand and curled herself around my neck, her usual favorite position.

"You live such a charmed life," I said, giving her a scratch and letting her sniff the ring from a distance. "Free food, travel, and all the back scratches you can ask for. Must be nice. I wish I had as little to worry about as you do."

That's when things started getting a little weird.

I should have taken the ring off. You know how you should never trust someone your dog can't stand? You should never wear a weapon, *or* fashion accessory, that your ferret doesn't like.

I know this now.

The ring began to shift on my finger, almost like it was being stretched and contorted from the inside, nestling flatter and flatter against my skin. My breath hitched as I stretched my arm out in front of me, putting as much space between myself and the ring as I possibly could. That was my cue to get the darned thing off. But it was getting smaller—contracting and bulging until it was tight against my skin.

I clawed at it with my right hand, desperate to get the freaky, writhing thing away from me.

But the ring was stuck tight to my finger, like it had been adhered with superglue. My whole arm began to ripple down to my elbow, making my stomach turn. Had the tech gotten under my skin? Had it infected me?

My entire body trembled, and my chest tightened. Pins and needles started in my toes and fingertips, and grew stronger until the pain was so extreme, my vision blurred red.

My skin—no, my entire body—was morphing and contracting.

"Guyyys!!" I wheezed. I needed help, and fast. *"Get down here!"* The words came out of me in harsh spasms, choked off by the lack of oxygen in my lungs. I couldn't get a good breath in. A boa constrictor of panic wrapped around me. I didn't have enough air to call out again.

The ring had grown to five times its size now, stretched flat along the entire length of my finger. Tendrils of gray metal began to sprout from its sides, weaving and crossing down my skin like a living spiderweb. Pickles gnawed at the material with all her strength, yanking and twisting, but it was no use.

She knew I was in trouble, too.

"Please—" I tried to stumble to the stairs to reach the others but crashed against the wall of the ship as I began to black out. "Pickles!" My breath was ragged. "Get them. Go get them. Find Mary." I hissed her name out like a command, desperate for my ferret to understand. But no, that wouldn't work. Mary was in the shower.

"F-find *Leo*!" I stammered.

Pickles, my noblest of tiny steeds, finally listened to me. She shot up the stairs to the ship's deck.

Seconds later, I fell to the ship's floor and knocked my hip against the hardwood. My last thought was of Pickles and her long, furry tail twisting like a kite behind her as she raced to find the others. Then everything went black.

So cliché, right? But trying on some sort of freaky ring that takes over your entire arm is a pretty scary thing. Blackouts are totally normal in that situation.

When I came to, the usual world had burned away and my vision was distorted, like a fun house mirror. I jerked my up head from the floor.

The chair in the barracks was at least ten times my height. In fact, the entire room seemed to have shifted on its axis. Everything was *huge*. The sleeping bunks. The bag of apples that sat by my backpack. Each apple was bigger than my head.

Oh my God, did I shrink down like Alice did in Wonderland?

I blinked several times and forced myself to look down at my feet. I needed to stabilize myself somehow.

"What. The—"

Two furry paws stared back at me.

Okay. Not Alice.

There was obviously something wrong here. Had the ring injected me with a hallucinogen? Maybe the ring incapacitated enemies by messing with their perception. I would be pretty easy to subdue right now. But getting a ring on someone else's finger could be difficult . . .

I needed more data to solve this equation.

"Tesla," I instructed myself. My voice sounded odd, a

little higher than normal and strained. I had to keep it together. "Move your left hand."

I obeyed myself, then watched in horror as the left paw in front of me started to move, the tiny, furry toes stretching and wiggling. My stomach tightened and my heart continued to race, betraying my fears.

"Now your right hand." I squeezed my eyes shut, then forced them open again. My left hand, or should I say *paw*, wiggled and shook.

"Am I a stinking *ferret*?!" I gasped. I scurried over to look at my reflection in the chair's metal legs and con-firmed my hypothesis. I was covered in fur like Pickles. And my coat was almost identical to hers: chocolate brown, misty gray, and white. I had two hind legs, with five toes and sharp claws on each.

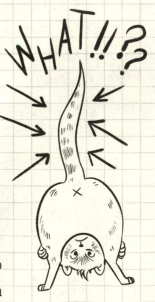

"Oh my God, is that . . . ?" I wriggled my rear end and nearly passed out again.

A fluffy tail, tapering off into a dainty white tip, stuck out from my behind.

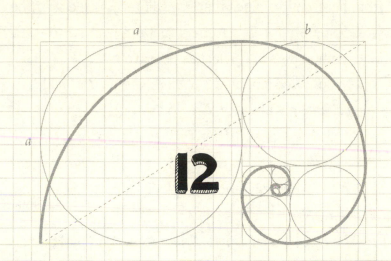

12

"Pickles!"

Leo's voice made my knees buckle with relief.

Yes! Leo could help!

I bounced up and down on my paws, readying myself to explain everything, and fast. The ring was messing with my head, but Leo hadn't touched it at all. He would see me as I really was, not as the ferret I was imagining.

He thumped down the stairs two at a time. His face was red from the sun, and his arms had already begun to tan from our time in the islands. Pickles weaved around his feet and bounded toward me, practically bowling me over. She wasn't attacking me or being rough: I could tell from her frantic whines that she still recognized me. She was desperate for Leo to help me and wanted to draw his attention my way as fast as possible.

"Nikki!" Leo shouted. "Where are you? Pickles is going absolutely bonkers. Are you all right?"

I rolled out from under Pickles and rushed over to Leo.

"Wait." He pivoted in place, pointing at me. "Pickles...?"

The real Pickles scurried over to us, and parked herself beside me.

And that moment—when Leo's mouth dropped open in a circle and his head tipped in confusion—*that's* when I knew how wrong I'd been.

"Why are there *two* of you?" he asked.

Shoot.

The ring hadn't made me hallucinate that I was a ferret. It had actually turned me *into* a ferret!

Two ferrets stared back at Leo.

Two Pickles.

One huge mystery.

Imagining yourself as a ferret is one thing, but... actually *being* one? That's enough to shock the speech out of you. How was I expected to string words together when I currently had a *tail*?

Leo frowned, kneeling down to timidly reach out to Pickles. Being a fellow genius, I knew exactly what thoughts swam through his head. He was thinking about the possibility that Pickles had been cloned.

It could happen, sure, with the right scientific procedures. But since Leo is no dummy, he would know that cloning takes time, and a whole laboratory of technology that we certainly didn't have on a ship in the Pacific Ocean. He also knew that I'd *never* clone Pickles. Why on earth would I want another crazy ferret running around me in the lab while I worked? One was difficult enough.

With cloning off the table, Leo would wonder if the ship was home to another ferret, who was coincidentally identical to Pickles. But given the fauna of the Galápagos, the odds of this were beyond improbable. Which would bring him to his final hypothesis: The ferret in front of him had gotten there by more mysterious means. I saw all of these options play out on his face, his expression full of confusion, fear, and intrigue.

He knelt down and spoke very slowly. "All right, twin Pickles. What is going on here?" He bit his lip and looked back and forth between me and the real Pickles, his face very pale all of a sudden.

Unfortunately for him, that's exactly when I got my voice back.

I stepped onto his shoe and glared at him. "Leo, it's me," I said.

Well, that did it.

Leo is a worldly kid and fluent in about thirty languages, but let me tell you, he was *not* prepared for a talking ferret.

He leaped back from me, grappling with the edge of the table to keep his balance. He opened his mouth, then closed it again. "Nikki?!" he hissed. Then he started searching the room, poking into cabinets, suitcases, and boxes.

I couldn't blame him. What I was asking his brilliant mind to believe wasn't possible.

Logically. Rationally. *Scientifically.*

There was no way that the voice he'd just heard—*my* voice—belonged to the ferret standing at his feet.

And yet.

I was officially a talking ferret.

"Is this a joke?!" His voice cracked in confusion. "Look, I know you're ticked off at us for making you shower last. Where are you?" He kept a wide berth between us, but Pickles nipped at his shoelaces in a rebellious attempt to keep him wrangled in the room with me.

I stepped forward. My brain hadn't quite figured out how to use four legs yet, so it was more of a stumble. My little ferret voice was sort of squeaky but still sounded remarkably like me (with a side of panic thrown in for good measure).

Leo blinked. "Ferrets can't imitate human speech. Am I cracking up? Maybe I'm getting that seasickness that makes sailors see mirages and mermaids and talking ferrets?" He swiped at his forehead, leaving his hair twisted in messy clumps.

"When was that last time I drank something?" he continued. "Am I dehydrated? Maybe I've got scurvy. No, I couldn't get scurvy after only a few days of travel." He was full-on babbling to himself now, ignoring me completely.

I tried to be patient with him, but the hysteria was wearing pretty thin. *He* wasn't the one who had turned into a ferret. So the least he could do was keep it together and help me.

"Leo!" I shouted. "Get ahold of yourself! It's *me*! I promise. I tried on the ring, and somehow . . . it changed me into *this*!"

He watched me, stunned. His chest was rising and falling fast. But he was listening. At least, I thought he was.

"Blink twice if you're with me here, Leo!" I instructed.

He blinked once, then shook his head as if to clear it before blinking again.

"I know ferrets can't imitate human speech," I continued in the slow voice I would use on a toddler. "But here I am, talking to you, aren't I? This doesn't make sense. But, Leo"—I hopped up onto his chest and stared him down—"you need to *help* me. You need to go upstairs. Tell the others what happened. We need everyone on this one, okay? Get Grace. Get all of them." I hoped I was coming across as stern and no-nonsense, but the adorable ferret face was probably throwing off my game.

Clenching my jaw, I begged
him. "We need to fix this.
Now."

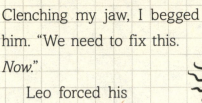

Leo forced his
mouth shut and cleared
his throat. "Right," he
said. "I'll get the
others. You're
going to be fine,
Tesla." He tried
to smile at me,
but the pitiful crack in his voice didn't inspire a lot of
confidence.

"Thank you," I said, planting my rear and letting my
long tail wrap around my feet.

"Uhh . . ." he started. A sheepish look crossed his face
and his cheeks went pink. "Nikki? You're gonna need to
get off me, first."

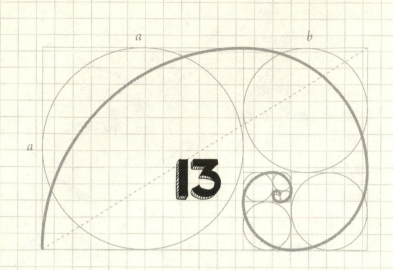

Mary was the first to make her way down the stairs. "Nikki, we're here. We came as fast as we—"

She stopped short in front of me, her hair still dripping from the shower. As the rest of the team crowded into the room behind her, Mary searched at eye level. Then her attention dropped to the floor, where I sat motionless.

"Oh." Her hand whipped up to cover her mouth. "Oh, dear."

"NIKKI IS A RODENT!" Mo's high-pitched shriek made everyone jump. He leaped away, grabbing Bert for protection. From what? From *me*.

Charlie squatted down and held out her hand to Pickles, who still sat protectively by my side. "Technically, ferrets are mustelids, not rodents. Nikki's probably so scared right now! Here, girl! It's okay!" She waved her hand at Pickles.

I rolled my ferret eyes and scurried up to Charlie. "That's Pickles, Charlie," I said. "*I'm* Nikki." I rose onto my hindquarters and batted her hand with my paw.

I have to hand it to Charlie—she handled our little high-five moment like a champ. The others were so thoroughly freaked out, I expected them to turn on their heels, march off the ship in single file, and hop into the ocean.

"Crikey, Nikki." Charlie lifted my paw. "And it was the ring that did this? Are you sure?"

I rolled my eyes. "No. I was getting bored waiting around for my shower, so I devised a secret and totally plausible experiment that, boom, turned me into a ferret while you all were getting lunch ready—*of course it was the ring, are you crazy?!*"

"All right, everyone," Grace said. She clapped her hands together and stood taller, lifting her chin. "I think we've seen enough. Whatever has happened to Nikki is our top priority."

She began pacing around us, whipping everyone out of their stupor. As she took her place at the front of the room, everyone instinctively shifted positions to form a semicircle around her, mimicking their seats in the Situation Room. With Martha away, Grace took her place in the central position.

A small flutter of relief grew inside me. If there was even a tiny sliver of a chance I could get back to my old self, these guys would find it.

"Brainstorm. Now," Grace said. "What have we got, and what do we do?"

Bert spoke first. "We need to figure out exactly how the ring works. What it does, other than turn our friends into ferrets."

Mo nodded. "Also who this tech belonged to in the first place."

"And how they were planning on using it," Grace added. "Before we were asked to secure it, that is. We need to know *everything* about it so we can make some sense of what's happened to Nikki. There has to be some explanation."

A stir of agreement circled the room, and I was eager to help them. But one thing was missing . . .

It was Mary—sweet, brilliant, empathetic Mary—who finally said the words I was desperate to hear.

"Um, guys?" She moved into the middle of the circle to sit cross-legged beside me, a show of solidarity and kindness. "I think we definitely need to figure out what the ring is, of course. But the first thing we need to do is get *Nikki* back. That has to be our priority."

It's a smile, I swear!

I gave her a small ferret smile. But it looked like I was baring my tiny little fangs at her, which caused her to jump back in alarm.

"Sorry!" I said, leaping

over to touch my paw to her knee. "Old habits. I was only trying to smile!"

Leo pinched his lips together. "Agreed. To get Nikki back, we need to know how we lost her in the first place. Retrace your steps, Nikki. Do you remember what happened before you changed? What you were doing?"

I shook my head. "I don't know. I mean, I put on the ring, but nothing happened right away. It was emitting a weird humming sound. And then it went berserk and started to . . . pulse. The metal flattened out and took over my hand, and my skin began to burn. The last thing I remember was seeing my skin ripple—which stung like heck—and then I blacked out!"

The others let out their breaths all at once, shoulders sinking.

"And nothing happened between you putting the ring on and turning into a . . . a mustelid?" Mary asked, darting a glance at Charlie.

"Nope," I said. I plunked down next to Pickles on the floor, suddenly feeling more tired than I'd ever been. Either it took a lot of energy to be a ferret, or the whole transformation was taking more of a toll on me than I realized. I leaned into Pickles's shoulder and yawned. She nuzzled her face into me protectively.

"Wait!" I said, hopping back up. "Pickles!"

Hearing her name made Pickles's ears perk up.

"What about her?" Grace asked.

"She started to freak out," I said. I waved my tiny paw in the air. "When I put on the ring, nothing happened. But within seconds, Pickles was right there, nipping at me and trying to tug it off. At the time I thought she was scared by the sound it made, but maybe . . ." I turned to Pickles, who was staring back at me with her bright chocolate brown eyes. "Maybe she knew the ring was bad news."

"Or maybe Pickles turned the tech on?" Bert asked. "Accidentally, of course. Could she have hit some kind of switch?" He mimicked pushing a fake button on his own hand.

"I didn't see anything like that." My whiskers drooped out of my eyeline as I frowned. "But . . ." I trailed off, pondering those last moments as a human.

The others perked up. "But what?" asked Mary.

I sniffed, suddenly feeling embarrassed. What had I said to Pickles just before the transformation happened? "I was jealous of her," I admitted, avoiding their eyes.

"Jealous? Of Pickles?" Grace made a face.

"I *might* have said that I wanted to be a ferret . . . ?" I shrugged, sending my furry shoulders near my ears.

"Why on earth would you want to be a ferret?" Charlie crossed her arms.

"Well, I didn't know this was going to happen, obviously!" I began pacing around Pickles. "I only said it as a joke! She lives a life of leisure—she's totally spoiled! I just said it in passing, but I think that may have been just before the transformation started."

Leo let out a loud whoosh of air. "Is it even possible?" he turned to Bert.

Bert blinked, and pointed at me. "She's a ferret, isn't she?"

"You know what I mean," Leo urged. "Nikki is still able to talk to us and speak English. She remembers all of us and has clearly retained all of her memories from before she became a ferret. Can *it* be possible?" he asked again.

Mary interrupted. "You're talking about cellular realignment?" Her face paled.

"Someone going to tell me what that is?" I whined, sinking to the floor.

Mary pinched her lips together before speaking, like she was weighing her words carefully. "History has been filled with stories of shape-shifters for as long as we've had stories themselves. It's possible that whoever invented this ring has found a way to *restructure* someone's body into a different shape."

My heart began to beat louder in my chest. "And it works by using the wearer's *thoughts*?" I asked. "Because I wanted to be a ferret? Or said it out loud?"

"It seems so, yes." Mary shook her head in a daze. "This ring makes a sought-after superpower a reality. Whoever wears the ring can turn into whatever they want they want. That *is* some pretty dangerous tech."

A beat of silence settled over the group, and the gravity of Mary's words crushed the air out of my lungs.

"So," Grace broke the silence. "I guess that means the million-dollar question is this: Nikki, have you considered *thinking* about being a human again?"

Unfortunately, I didn't get a chance to answer her.

Why?

Because that's when the ship exploded.

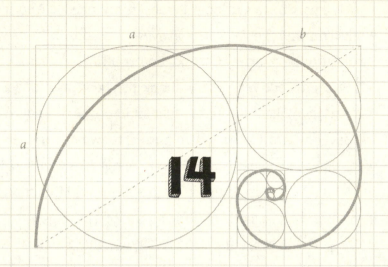

14

Once, when I was a little kid, I accidentally blew up the tub in our bathroom. I was mixing some chemicals to see what would happen. (How *else* was I going to find out?) One minute, I was pouring a beaker of green liquid into a test tube; the next, I was lying on my back in a pile of burnt wood and wet puddles.

That's what it felt like when our ship, or, rather, the ship we had *borrowed*, went up in a smoky, clanging, soppy blaze.

Dust billowed in clouds around me, and the sound of cracking planks made my eardrums quake. There was no sign of where the explosion had started. The belly of the ship was unharmed, but the unmistakable tang of smoke and salt stung my eyes. Had a grenade detonated on the main deck?

"Someone's here!" Charlie bellowed. "Protect Nikki!"

Leo scrambled to his feet and yanked me up to his shoulder by the scruff of my neck. I would have been peeved at how unceremoniously he was handling me, but we had bigger fish to fry. And by "fish," I mean "armed robbers."

Three men in all-black outfits thundered down the stairs. They held guns close to their chests. Grace and the others moved fast, shifting protectively around each other. But instead of taking his usual place next to Mo, Leo dove for the closet. In the murky dust, I clung tightly to him as he used his legs to brace himself in the tiny space and slammed his shoulder against the ceiling.

An escape hatch. He was leaving the others behind.

"What are you doing?!" I yelled at him. My eyes watered at the bright sunlight filtering in through the crawl space. How had he known the ship had a secret hatch to the main deck in the closet?

He ignored me, bolting down the deck at a breakneck pace. His sneakers skidded against the wet planks until he reached the mast.

"Hang on," he whispered. He spit in his palms and began climbing the mast, clearly headed for the small barrel-shaped crow's nest at the top. Proper sailors would have used this nest as a lookout, but I hadn't given it a second thought. He scaled the mast in a few moments, then hoisted his leg over the top of the lookout. Panting with exertion, he ducked his head out of sight and caught his breath.

"Why did you bring us up here?" I scurried off his neck to sit on his knee and glare at him. "Everyone is fighting down there and you abandon them?!" I shook my head in disgust. If I had to scramble down the mast and fight these goons alone, I was ready for it.

"No!" Leo ordered. He whipped his hand out to block me from leaving. "You can't! *Listen!*"

The commotion on deck got louder.

"Where is it?!" a voice shouted. It had to be one of the robbers. "Give it to us now, and nobody gets hurt!"

Leo's eyes widened and he crouched lower. "Nikki! Get down!"

"We don't know what you're talking about!" That one was Grace. Whatever was happening to the team down there, I could tell from her voice that they were scared, but nobody was hurt.

Yet.

"We have to help them!" I begged. "They're in trouble. Those guys have guns!" I moved again to dash away, crossing my paws that I would somehow be able to manage the steep descent of the tall mast.

"Stay here, Nikki!" Leo let me peek my head over the crow's nest to see the scene below, but one inch farther earned me a poke in the shoulder. "Hey! Get *down*! Are you trying to be seen, or what?!"

"No, Leo!" I screamed, and nipped at his hand. "Our friends need us!"

"Don't you get it?" Leo hissed. "We *can't* let them capture you! They're looking for the ring. The last thing we need is for that cellular-realignment technology to fall into the hands of guys with guns. Trust me!"

Can ferrets cry? It was a question I'd never considered before, but one that I had the answer to pretty quickly. Leo and I hid out in the crow's nest above the ruckus as the intruders continued their assault. It was heartbreaking to hear my friends in such dire trouble and to do nothing to help them. By the sounds of the loud crashes and splintering wood below, the men in black were ransacking the ship, searching for the ring in every possible hiding spot, every nook and cranny. But Leo's instincts seemed to be sharp—nobody thought to look up where we were hidden, above the fray.

"It's not here!" another voice bellowed out, and was immediately followed by a loud *thwap*.

"Of course it is! Get out of the way, Stretch!" a third man yelled.

I cringed at the thought of Bert facing his assailant, who no doubt had a gun trained on him.

"Out of the way, I said!" the voice bleated again. "You three—beat it, or you'll regret it!"

My friends were helpless down there, but nobody made a move to reveal where Leo and I were hiding. Would I be that brave in the same situation? A sudden chorus of protest had my fur standing on end.

"You! Out of the way, kid!" A lone burst of gunfire rang out, and I clutched Leo's shoulder in terror, straining to hear the voices of everyone I cared about. Had someone been *shot*?

"They're okay." Leo wiped the sweat from his face and continued to peer down at the scene. "One of those dudes shot the side of the ship."

If only that had made me feel any better. Whatever the man had in his sights, he wasn't taking no for an answer.

A quieter voice cut through the commotion. I couldn't make out the words, but I was certain from the muffled lilt that it was Mary.

Loud crashing below us made my heart plummet. "Leave her alone!" Charlie's and Grace's shrieks gave away the truth. "She doesn't have it!"

"Oh no," Leo breathed out, shaking his head as he watched.

"What?!" I tried desperately to get a better view, but he kept shoving me back to safety.

"It's Mary." Leo's face twisted with pain as he listened to the whole thing unfold below. "She's pointing to a small dinghy docked next to the ship. Probably the one those creeps came on."

I squeaked with panic. "What on earth could she

have to say to them? Why are the others even letting her get so close?"

Something was very wrong. The men with guns had ceased their yelling, and instead, their voices were low and measured. Was Mary trying to reason with them?

Beside me, Leo fidgeted, almost like he was trying to stop himself from standing and rushing to her aid. His hands flexed and stretched automatically, and he gripped his knees hard.

"Don't do it, Mary," he whispered.

"Don't do *what*?" I demanded. I poked my nose up over the crow's nest to get a better look.

Mary's hands were now bound behind her, and the three men were leading her to the side of the ship.

Leo forced his eyes shut, and his voice cracked as he spoke. "They're taking her with them."

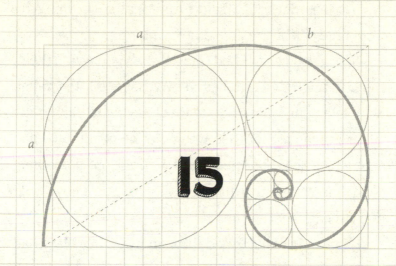

15

"What do we do, Leo?!" I cried. "We have to help her!" The back of my throat seared with pain at the thought of my best friend being taken by these awful men.

Leo's defeated, sunken expression was numbing. He knew what I didn't want to accept. My attention moved to the dinghy the men were leading her toward, then to a speedboat listing in the water a couple hundred yards away.

Those men thought she either had the ring or knew where it was secured. Had she told them as much?

"We can't do anything, Nikki," he said. He opened his eyes and lifted his face to the sky, listening intently below. "If they find me, they find you. I can't risk it. Mary must know what she's doing."

"No, she doesn't!" I said. "And neither do we! Why would she risk her life for some dumb ring?"

"Don't you get it?!" Leo said. "If she's going with them, she *does* think it's worth her life! We have to listen to her. She's telling us what to do without saying it. Taking the fall so we can escape. She would not be going if she had another choice. She must have figured out something about these men or why they're here. You know what Mary is like."

Rage and guilt stormed through me. Sure, Mary had a knack for reading people and their actions. But this? It was much too dangerous.

I let out a small whimper as I watched Mary board the dinghy. Her face was a mask of indifference. Whatever these men wanted with her, she wasn't going to give in. Admiration and pride swelled through me, but it was tainted by the massive tsunami of shame I felt. It was my fault that she was being captured. All because I was dumb enough to try on a ring—a *weapon*—I didn't understand. And now Mary was paying the price.

Waves crisscrossed out behind them as the dinghy sputtered its way to the larger speedboat. From there, Mary was only visible for a few seconds before she disappeared from view.

Soon, the only sounds I could hear were the lapping water and gentle thumps below as the team assessed the damage. Everyone was uninjured, except for a few bumps and bruises. Nobody spoke. I wanted to hide in the crow's nest for the rest of my life. Anything to avoid facing the others.

But I wasn't going to stop until Mary was home safe, and I was useless as a ferret.

I needed to be *myself* to help her.

A faint tingle began to spread out over my body, and immediately my attention leaped to our earlier conversation about how the ring worked. Was it responding to my thoughts right now? Is that why my toes and fingertips were burning? I tried to focus my thoughts, willing every cell of my body to return to its usual self. Closing my eyes, I envisioned looking in a mirror and seeing my own face staring back at me, then let the image drop down past my neck to the rest of my body, right down to my toes.

I *had* to get this right. Mary's life depended on it.

"Hey," Leo said, leaning away from me and giving me some air. "Are you okay?"

The transformation happened quickly this time, with only a little spark of pain. One minute I was a ferret, clinging to the wooden lip of the crow's nest with tiny claws. The next? I was myself again, bonking my human-sized knee against the side of the crow's nest.

I squeezed my hands together—actual flesh and blood hands with fingernails and zero fur—and let out an enormous sigh. Then I patted my face and arms to be certain. Everything felt normal.

"Holy moly," Leo said, blinking fast. "You're back!"

I should have been ecstatic: I was human again! But the pain of losing Mary was too much. I wanted nothing more than to get started on our plan to rescue her.

"I'm back," I croaked. My voice was scratchy and raw. "I don't exactly know how this thing works yet, but picturing myself as human again seemed to activate the ring's capabilities."

My legs buckled as I tried to climb out of the crow's nest, so I leaned on Leo for a moment.

"Take it off." Leo pointed to my finger. Now that I was myself again, the ring sparkled in the setting sun. "We don't want any other accidental ferret transformations."

I couldn't agree more. Yanking the ring from my finger, I resisted the urge to chuck the thing into the ocean, never to be seen again.

"Come on." He held out his hand to help me from our perch. "Take your time, you've been through a lot."

I shook my head angrily. "We don't *have* time," I said. "Mary needs us. We need a plan."

"Nikki!" Charlie rushed over to me when I set foot on the deck. "You're back! I thought we were up the creek on that one! Thank God Leo got you out of there in time." She and Mo wrapped me in a hug while Bert patted my shoulder awkwardly.

"I'm fine," I mumbled. Opening my mouth broke the dam inside of me. Guilt started to pour out. "I'm so sorry, everyone," I said. "This is all my fault. I shouldn't have touched the ring. I should have waited to have my shower like everyone else, and Mary would still be safe."

A shadow crossed over Grace's face, and she curled her lip in disgust. "Hold up." She looked beyond us. "It ain't over!"

She rushed over to the rail of the ship. I followed her, urging my feet to do as they were told. They were still a little wobbly, probably because I had just gotten used to having four feet, rather than two.

Dusk had painted the sky with gorgeous purples, oranges, and reds, but there was nothing beautiful about the sight below: Another boat was approaching. A small speedboat, with a lone figure parked right in the middle. Judging by the wide shoulders and loose, shaggy hair, it was a man.

"Positions, everyone," Grace instructed.

"We can't just let him come aboard!" Bert said, crossing his arms over his chest.

"Oh, he's coming aboard, all right," Grace responded. "But this time, we're not getting ambushed."

As the man maneuvered closer, his voice rang out. "I'm unarmed!"

"Oh, well, that changes everything." Bert perched his hands on his hips in exasperation. "Let's invite him up for some tea, then! Charlie, go put your kettle on! Someone round up some biscuits!"

Grace shushed him, but I had to agree with Bert on this one. The odds that this man was bringing us good news were slim.

"I'm coming up!" he yelled again. "Please, don't shoot."

Bert made a face. "Shoot?" he mouthed. "Who the heck is this guy?"

"We've got a sniper in the crow's nest if you feel like trying anything!" Charlie quipped. It was a convincing enough lie that I looked above us without thinking.

Two hands gripped the railing. The man climbed up a small ladder that he had brought in his own dinghy. His white linen shirt was rumpled and stained, and his arms were deeply tanned.

"Who are you?" Grace barked.

He smiled weakly at us. His hair was a messy chestnut brown mop, and his dark eyes crinkled at the corners, giving him an air of exhaustion. He extended his hands in front of him, like he was offering an apology.

"Thank you for letting me board." His voice was scratchy. Who knows how long he'd been in the water to reach us. Deep rivers of dirt and sweat lined his face. But there was also something unsettling about him. Something I couldn't quite place. Was it the relaxed way his shoulders drooped, when he should have been nervous? Or the hint of a satisfied smile that barely graced his lips? He seemed *eager*. But at the same time, incredibly tired and unsure.

I edged farther away from him.

"I'm here to help," he continued. "I know you broke into the cave vault. I know your friend was kidnapped a few moments ago. And I know that is no normal ring you've got." He raised a long, shaky fingertip and pointed it directly at me.

I wish I could say we had some clever response to that, but we didn't. Instead, we stood there, wavering slightly as the ship bobbed side to side, while this random dude threw down a bunch of truth at our feet.

Grace, always on target, was first to speak. "And how do you know that, huh?" She threw him a bottle of water. An offering.

He caught the bottle in one hand and cranked off the lid, draining it with one long gulp. A stream of water dripped from his chin, and in that moment, with the back of his hand casually wiping his mouth, the truth crashed into me like a rogue wave.

I knew exactly why I found him so troubling . . .

"Answer me." There was more than a note of warning in Grace's words. "How do you know about us?"

The bottle dropped to the deck as the man inspected each of us. By the time he got to me, that tiny smile began to appear again. Quirked at the edges and slightly crooked.

Familiar.

He shrugged and scratched the back of his head. "Because I designed the vault. And that ring? The silver ring that just turned Nikki into a ferret? I invented that, too."

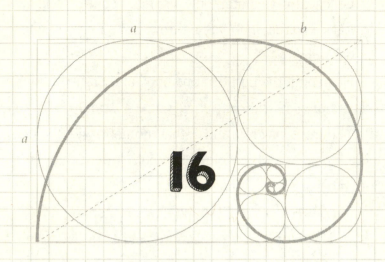

16

Despite the seven years that had passed, I still recognized him. He had changed, of course. His face was weathered. His eyes a gray that seemed darker than I remembered. And his tattered shirt made him look more like a lost tourist than a scientist.

But it was definitely him.

"Dad?" I said. I leaned against a deck chair for support. Anything to keep me upright while my knees were quaking with confusion. The murmurs of the team grew around us, but I was too busy with my own storming thoughts to worry about what they thought.

"Nikki," he said. His shoulders sagged with relief. He smiled at me, but he didn't open his arms for a hug. It's a good thing, too, because I might have taken the opportunity to push him right into the ocean. "We've got a lot of catching up to do."

I couldn't control myself; I was already shaking my head in anger. My throat trembled as I struggled to hold back tears. "Not interested."

"Nikki." Grace glanced at the others. Uncertain, maybe for the first time, of what to do. "Why don't we—"

"No!" I shouted, interrupting her. My hearing started to get fuzzy. All of my blood was rushing to my head, and I was close to hyperventilating. "No! He does not get to just show up like this!" I turned around to face him. "*No! Get back into your stupid boat and row away or what-ever, but never, ever come back!*"

Dad's mouth clamped shut. "I understand." He continued to watch me, ignoring the others. "You're upset. I know I deserve every ounce of your anger, but right now you all must listen to me."

I'd already started to march away, but it turned into more of a pace when I realized there was no way to truly disappear off this dumb ship. I considered jumping into the ocean myself, just to get away from him. Leo side-stepped out of my way, probably afraid I'd knock him over the railing.

"We *all* need to get off the ship." Dad gestured to the

horizon and a set of moving lights on the main island. Flashlights? A car?

"Do you see those lights? A group of scientists owns this ship. I spoke with them earlier, and they're on their way back here as we speak. Do you want them to discover you've hijacked their ship for the day for a joyride up the coastline? I don't think they'll be pleased to see all the damage." He flicked his gaze to the broken railing on the stairs that descended into the belly of the ship. "They'll call the Coast Guard, and you'll be too busy answering questions to help your kidnapped friend. But I'm offering my services—I know where they took her."

"Give us a minute." Grace opened her arms and waved us all in close. She kept her voice barely above a whisper. "He's right. Nikki, I know this is hard for you. But we *do* need to get off this ship right now. If he knows about the ring, he's probably telling the truth about tracking whoever took Mary. He could help us find her . . ."

"He's a *criminal*." I couldn't believe Grace was even considering listening to him. "He's done nothing to show us we can trust him."

Bert poked his head out of our circle to look at my dad again. "Well, he did warn us about the scientists returning . . . I think maybe he wants to help."

I scoffed. "He's worried about himself. Can't we call Martha? She'll have a better idea."

Grace's mouth set in a tight line. "I tried. I can't get ahold of her. Either we're out of range, or the explosion from the ambush messed with our radio signal. I can send her an email once we get some Wi-Fi, but we can't exactly stick around to wait for her right now."

My stomach sank.

"Is Mary worth the risk?" Grace asked suddenly, facing me with fierce eyes.

Her question stopped me short. "You know I'd do anything for Mary," I said. "I just don't think my dad will help."

Grace bit her lip. "And I think you're not seeing clearly because of how upset you are with him." She held up her hand when she saw me begin to protest. "And you're entitled to be angry! But if we let your past with him interfere with what's in front of us right *now*, we might regret it. Think of how distracted you've been lately! Nobody's blaming you, but we need to be logical here, Nik. Mary's in trouble, and this guy—your father—knows where she is."

Shame spread over me like fire. They thought my judgment was clouded by anger? Doubt clung to my chest, making it hard to breathe all of a sudden. Were they right?

No.

There was no way that Dad was trustworthy.

But he did have information. And if spending time with him meant we had even a slim chance to get her back, I knew what we had to do.

"Okay," I said. "For Mary, then."

"So we're agreed?" Grace put her hands on her hips. "We leave right now. We can make shelter on the island. If we wait until morning, we could—"

"Uh, if I may?" Dad's voice made us all jump. He'd

edged his way between Mo and Leo, leaning in and whispering like he was part of our circle. "You don't want to be spending the night in the dark without food or water. I've got a laboratory in Ecuador, near the Cotopaxi volcano. And a plane to get us there. You'll be safe, and we can sort out what to do next. You *do* want to get your friend back, right?"

I gawked at him, disgusted. Secret laboratories? Volcanoes? How could anyone even consider trusting him? He was basically the villain from every spy movie I'd ever seen.

Dad stepped out of the way to let us talk again, but I could already tell from Grace's expression that it had been decided. I was outvoted on this.

Charlie patted my arm. "We need him to get us over to the mainland so we can figure out how to save Mary. We'll all be watching him constantly. Right, guys?"

Leo nodded brusquely. "We got your back, Nik."

"Then it's done," Grace said, snapping up to her full height. We faced my dad, who had busied himself staring out at the water, pretending he wasn't listening.

But of course he was.

"This plane of yours," Grace said, "where is it? Does it have enough room? And do you have a pilot?

Will we be meeting any *other* new faces today?" She barely kept the sarcasm out of her voice.

Dad smiled, and the familiar shape of his crooked left incisor cemented itself into my mind, mingling with memories I didn't realize I still had. A million smiles, all for me as a kid.

"It's a few hundred yards inland," Dad answered. "And yes, there's room for us all."

"And where's the pilot?" Grace asked.

Dad winked at me. "You're looking at him."

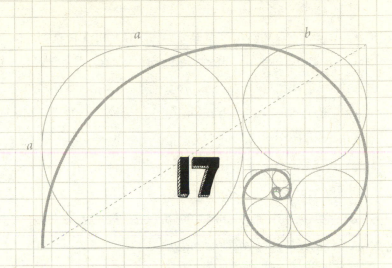

17

You know how you always want to yell at the people in horror movies? The ones who traipse upstairs looking for the killer when they should be running as fast as they can from the house and not looking back?

That is how I felt stepping into the stainless steel elevator that would take us down into the depths of Dad's secret laboratory, with him by our side.

"Dude," Bert said. His Adam's apple bobbed up and down as he swallowed, inspecting the ceiling of the elevator. "I thought you said your lab was near the Cotopaxi volcano . . . not *in* it." He held the collar of his shirt open to cool off. "Are you sure this thing isn't active right now?" He touched the side of the elevator walls with the back of his hand, testing the temperature.

Dad didn't answer at first. I shouldn't have been surprised to see the elevator was hidden among the rocks of
the Cotopaxi volcano, shrouded with foliage. There was
no building or parking lot. Instead, his lab was built
directly into the rocks, hidden within the jungle. Did he
actually build this himself? Or had he discovered it and
taken over the space, like we had with the ship?

"I like my privacy," he replied.

Or maybe, I thought smugly, *because he was wanted by
police, he had to fly under the radar.*

"Here we are," Dad said. The elevator door yawned
open, revealing his laboratory. We stepped out cautiously,
letting our vision adjust to the dim lights.

"It's not much, but it's home." Dad spread his arms
out to welcome us, with a slight grimace on his face. "At
least, home on this continent."

I clenched my jaw at his comment, which had done
nothing but remind me of the home—*our* home—that
he'd left behind.

A row of lab benches flanked each side of the
space, and gray shelves lined every wall. Flickering
lights suspended on electrical cords hung above our
heads, peppering the ceiling like huge fireflies. The
place wasn't exactly tidy, but there seemed to be an
order to everything. But there was another quality to

the space, as well: It was temporary. Bandages of masking tape bound many of the table legs, and the walls had been haphazardly painted in various shades of white and gray, as though the owner of the space couldn't decide what color he really wanted. Or maybe he didn't care.

This wasn't a place to live.

It was a place to hide.

I let my glance drift to the messiest desk, which was strewn with notepads and diagrams and the hurried scribbles of an inventor at work. A single framed photograph rested on the left, next to a pile of nubby pencils and crumpled scraps.

My mother's face beamed back at me. And four- or five-year-old me, tucked under the crook of her arm. A burst of renewed annoyance surged through me. What right did he have to keep our picture out like that? Like we were some long-lost happy family?

No one was smiling now.

We dropped our belongings in one corner of the room while Leo and Bert organized some chairs for us all in the middle of the space. A sharp pang of panic shot through me when I noted that they'd set out a chair for Mary without thinking. She was always so quiet and even-tempered, never one to get overly excited or in your

face. And yet, the group felt oddly lifeless without her—
like we were missing our heart.

"Here." Dad handed me two small metal bowls, nestled together.

I stepped back from his offering. "What's this?"

He nodded to Pickles, who was protectively curled
around my neck and hadn't moved since the flight here.
"For your ferret. She must be getting hungry and thirsty
by now," he said. "I've got some crackers on that top shelf,
and there's some cheese in the fridge. Feel free to make a
plate for yourselves, too."

Crackers and cheese. Another memory. Dad always used to cut up cheese for me in tiny cubes at lunchtime, so I could stack them on my crackers before eating them. We called it *cheese castle*. The memories felt jagged in my mind, and being around him was starting to feel like navigating a floor covered in broken glass. Exactly how many memories did I have hidden away? And here I thought I barely remembered him. It turns out I did—he was just buried under years of hatred. How many times had he made me lunch before he left us?

"Hey, Tesla!" Someone snapped their fingers near my ear. "Earth to Nikki . . ."

I blinked back to reality to face Bert, whose eyebrow was quirked with concern. "Watch your toes." He gestured to the chair he was shuffling by my feet.

"Huh? S-s-sorry," I stammered. I shook my head to shoo away the memories. If I wanted to get Mary back, I'd need to stay sharp, not buried in the past.

I cautiously took the bowls from Dad and turned them over in my hand. Pickles *was* starving, but I didn't want him to think two bowls were going to fix the chasm between us.

"Thanks for letting us stay here, Mr. . . . Mr. . . ." Bert struggled for the name.

Tesla, of course, was my mother's last name, which we'd adopted after Dad left us. My father's real name was—

"Faraday," Dad responded. "You can call me Mike."

"Mike," Leo repeated. He stretched out his hand to shake Dad's. "I'm Leo da Vinci."

I scoffed. Leo the traitor.

It was hard enough looking him in the eye, but seeing all my friends be civil and polite to him? Falling for his tricks? That was *maddening*.

"Nice to meet you, Leo," Dad said. "I'm sorry that we have to meet under these circumstances. Please, let's all take a seat. We've got a lot to cover."

"If you don't mind, Mike," Grace said. "We need to get working on a plan to retrieve Mary. We appreciate you lending us the space, but every passing minute means there's less of a chance we'll get her back." Grace took her seat and waited for everyone to do the same.

"Agreed." Dad scratched the scruff on his chin and gave me an apologetic look. "But there's something you need to know."

"And what's that?" Grace could barely hide her impatience. Her ankle bounced at top speed on her knee.

Dad's face was grim. He reached into his pocket and removed a small black remote. Aiming it at a blank screen to his left, he clicked once, and the monitor flickered to life.

A spotty image reflected back at us, knitting together first in snowy gray shimmers, then finally settling into clarity. A girl sitting in a chair in an empty white room. Her hair was messy as though she hadn't had a chance to tidy it after a long trip. Her hands were folded gently in her lap.

Mary.

I jumped to my feet, pointing an accusing finger at the screen. In an instant, all the doubts I'd had about my father rose up in my throat.

"You see?!" I shouted. "He *is* in on it!

Grace's eyes were fierce, but she didn't make a move. The others shifted in their chairs, waiting for her to respond. Meanwhile, I was eyeballing the door, ready to make a run for it.

Dad set the remote down. "I know how it looks," he explained. "But you're going to have to trust me here. I was the one who arranged for you to be here today, to break into my vault and steal the ring."

Instantly, my thoughts shot back to the cave. It had been programmed to respond to the sound of *my* voice. And that *Alice's Adventures in Wonderland* connection . . . How had he known I would remember him reading me that story?

"Why?" Grace's voice dropped and her knuckles turned white as she gripped the side of her chair. She kept sneaking glances at Mary on the screen. "Why try to kill us?"

"I wasn't trying to kill anyone. If I'd truly wanted any of you dead, I've had several chances."

A quiet murmur circled the room as the others reluctantly conceded the point. I wasn't so sure though. Dad was unpredictable.

He let that settle over us before continuing. "I had to see if my assumptions about you all were correct," he said. "I've been following Nikki for years. From a distance, of course. I observed her strengths and her passions. And when she joined Genius Academy, I was happy to see she'd found some friends who would understand her."

I glared at him. "So getting us to steal the ring was a test? One you concocted because *you* decided you wanted to have me in your life again, out of nowhere."

"It's been so hard watching from the sidelines," he said. "I've seen you grow up without me, followed your progress at every school you attended or tutor you worked with. I know that I've caused you more trouble than I could ever apologize for. But it's *time*, Nikki. Time for us to mend what's broken between us."

Everybody else remained silent.

"And why's that, huh?" I demanded. My hands began to shake with anger. Pickles scurried down to them, checking my fingers. Poor thing probably thought I was turning into a ferret again. But this? There was no science involved at all.

Just anger.

"The man who kidnapped your friend wants that ring for himself," Dad said. "And I need your help to stop him. I have a plan." He lifted his head with a hint of pride. "But it's going to take each of you for it to work."

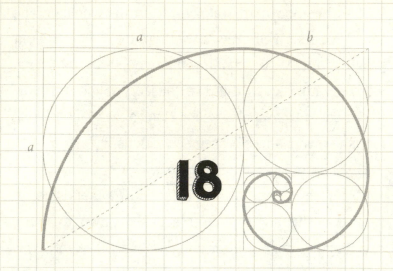

18

"You want *our* help?!" I couldn't stop the words from tumbling out. All this nonsense about working together and my broken heart about Mary's kidnapping mingled together in a toxic mix of resentment.

"Do I need to remind you why you're even *here*? Underground and hiding?!" I demanded. "It's because you blew up your laboratory seven years ago, remember? Because I do. The police found plans for an explosive that you were going to use to hurt people. And now you expect me and my friends to trust you?! You're the reason Mary got kidnapped. She's even on *your* screen right now. For all we know, you planned this whole thing!"

I grabbed a glass of water and took an angry gulp, desperate to soothe my cracking, hoarse throat. I should have been embarrassed of his horrible past. But unlike every other time it had come up, this time telling the truth in front of everyone made me feel stronger.

He straightened out his ruffled shirt. "I promise you—"

"I don't *want* your promises!" I said. And this is where everything went wrong.

You see, there's a rule about laboratories: You don't touch *anything* if you don't know what it is. Dad's laboratory shelves were lined with beakers and jars filled with various colored liquids and who knows what else. I should have known better.

But in my fit of anger, I didn't set my glass down carefully on the table like I should have. Instead, I whirled around and smacked it down hard on the shelf by my elbow, next to some small beakers.

Like I said, sometimes you do dumb things when you're mad.

The glass shattered, and I jerked my arm away to avoid getting cut, sending a beaker tumbling to the ground. The beaker smashed in the puddle of spilled water, and sizzling gray smoke erupted from the ground like a miniature geyser, shooting hot splatters through the air. It all happened so fast, I wasn't able to dive in front of Grace before it was too late.

"Ow!" she yelped. "What the heck, Nikki?!" Her mouth dropped open in shock as she cradled her wrist, where the chemicals had splashed her. She sucked in a fast breath, shaking her hand in pain. "Ow, ow, *oww* . . . !"

Dad leaped from his chair and was at her feet within seconds. "Hold still," he said. "The beaker had water-reactive material in it. *Don't* touch it!"

"Oh my God, Grace," I said, rushing over and

gripping her shoulder. I inspected her face for any other spatters or burns, but all the damage seemed to be on her wrist, where a quarter-sized splatter of red marks was blistering on her skin. "I'm so sorry! I didn't even see!" The puddle of sizzling chemicals hissed beside me, but Leo quickly covered the whole mess with a thick towel he found on a nearby shelf.

Dad pointed to Bert. "You. On the shelf beside the fridge. Find the mineral oil. It's in a bottle with a blue lid," he barked.

Bert did as he asked and returned a few moments later, shoving a bottle into my father's hands. Within a few minutes, Dad had bandaged up Grace's wrist, and in the time it took to fix her up, my anger had shrunk from a lion's roar to a kitten's mew—I was embarrassed about my outburst.

I'd messed up. *Again*.

"I'm *so* sorry," I repeated.

Grace waved her good hand dismissively, but it was easy to read the leftover pain behind her tight smile. "It's fine, Nikki. I know it was an accident."

I hugged her, furious with myself for such a stupid mistake. The guilt became even worse when my mind flashed to our last meeting with Martha. Back at the Academy, the whole team had thought I was distracted

by the news that my dad was still alive, and here I was knocking over dangerous chemicals in *his* laboratory and hurting one of my best friends. No matter how much I tried to push my past away—to freeze it where it couldn't hurt me—the ice of my memories kept cracking and shattering around me.

Watching Dad tend to Grace's injury didn't make it any easier either. He spoke gently and kindly, and assured her that she'd be okay the whole time he worked.

How could someone who had done such horrible things be so, well . . . *nice*?

Usually, when I faced a tricky problem in the lab, I trusted my instincts. But what if my instincts were too . . . raw? Like the chemical reaction that had burned Grace's arm, I felt sizzling and shaky in my own skin, and there was nothing I could use to neutralize it.

When Grace was settled and bandaged, Dad wiped his hands on a clean towel and turned to me. He looked as emotionally exhausted as I felt, sending another twinge of doubt through me.

"I know I have a lifetime of things to explain to you." He slumped down his chair and leaned forward, letting his head hang down. "But let's start with the ring. Okay?"

His gentle demeanor made my ears burn with shame. Here, I was breaking beakers, while he stayed perfectly calm. I hadn't realized it, but I'd been experimenting with those painful memories, and trying to bury the past in my laboratory drawers hadn't exactly produced the results I'd been hoping for. If I wanted a different outcome, I would need to try something different. And that meant giving my dad a chance, just this once.

"Okay," I said, forcing myself to look him in the eye. "I'm listening."

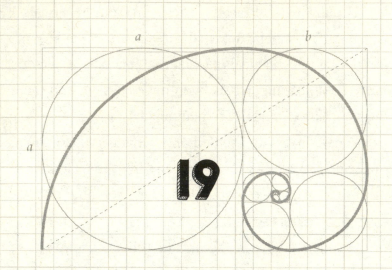

a b

a

19

When I was little, Dad used to tuck me in with a bedtime story every night. He'd do voices and try to skip pages to see if I'd notice (I always did), and when he was finished, I'd beg him to read me one more.

I didn't remember any of this until he started to speak in a strong, clear voice. "Eight or nine years ago, I devised the ring's technology. It started as simple curiosity. You all understand, of course." He glanced up at the group. "Sometimes you experiment to see if a crazy idea will work. To find the limits of what's possible."

Grace nudged me with her good arm and let out the smallest hint of a sour laugh. "Sound familiar?"

I clamped my lips together and kept listening.

"At first," he continued, "it was just a pet project that allowed me to explore something new. There was very little research about cellular realignment out there, and none of it was promising. But my colleague Dr. Joseph Nolan encouraged me to continue. I thought he was trying to cheer me up, to convince me that my research wasn't useless." A soft smile crossed his face. "Of course, now I know better."

"So you got it to work," Leo said. "Cellular realignment."

Dad nodded. "I had to get it wrong three hundred and sixty-eight times before I got it right though. It was the nanomachines, you see. They were crucial. Once I realized I could use them to commandeer your own cells and convince them to act as changeable stem cells, everything fell into place."

Leo glanced at me in wide-eyed amazement.

"And that's when things went south," Dad said. "Nolan had been hanging around the lab while I was working. When I managed to finish the prototype, a ring, he started to turn. He had started out his career as a promising mind who wanted to help the world through technology. He was a little younger than me, and I think he saw me as a mentor early on. But he became sneaky and obsessed with his own cleverness. And soon, I caught him stealing bits of my research. He was trying to piece together how I'd harnessed cellular realignment. At that point I didn't have a working prototype of the tech, but I was close."

"Whoa," Bert said. "Some friend."

"Right." Dad raised his eyebrows. "But we *were* friends for years. Because of that, I thought I could confront him. I wanted to give him the benefit of the doubt. For him to be honest about what he was doing. And he was honest, all right." Dad laughed bitterly.

"What did he say?" Charlie asked. I tried not to take it personally that the team was hanging on to my dad's every word. Like it or not, he was good at holding attention.

"He said that he had a buyer." Dad held up his hands in frustration. "He wanted to sell my ring's technology to the highest bidder. Promised me we could work together and split the profit."

"Why didn't you?" I asked bluntly. "I bet you could get a fortune for something like this."

Confusion clouded his face. "Because Nolan didn't care what the tech would be used for. That it could be a weapon unlike any other. You turned into a ferret, Nikki, but in the wrong hands, a ring like this could turn anyone into a lethal monster. And a large number of the rings?

Imagine what they could do for the military of a country at war . . ."

He went to his desk, where he sifted through cream-colored folders until he found what he was looking for. "This is what the wearer can become, if they're trained properly." He dropped the folder onto my lap. "I'm sorry," he added, pursing his lips together. "It's not for the faint of heart."

I gingerly lifted the top flap and gasped at the first page inside. Black-and-white photos of vicious creatures screamed at me from the pages, blood as dark as ink dripping from their teeth. Animals with twisted jaws, thick, curving claws, and raggedy fur. The others clustered around me while Dad began to pace.

"These don't look like any animal I recognize," Charlie whispered.

"That's because they're not normal animals." Dad's face had paled. "My surveillance tells me Nolan has been experimenting to find out how far the tech can change the human body. There aren't limits for a skilled user. A person wearing the ring can become any kind of monster they can imagine. If he sells it, a truly evil person could make an army of monsters."

I flipped through the images, my skin crawling more with every page turn. But something tugged at my

attention even more than the horrific pictures. Why would one monster care about stopping another?

It didn't make sense.

"So?" I said, slamming the folder shut. I ignored the harsh looks from the others, and stayed as calm as I could. All I wanted were answers. "The type of guy who makes plans to hurt innocent people and abandons his family wouldn't care if his technology was used for war. Even if it meant monsters like this."

Dad sucked in a breath. "No, you're right. That type of man wouldn't blink at it."

Leo broke the silence that followed, trying to get us

back on track. "So Nolan wanted to sell the ring as a weapon, and you said no."

"I did," Dad confirmed. "I told him that there was no way I would hand over the prototype or any of my research. That he was on his own."

"What happened then?" Charlie chewed on her ragged fingernails as she spoke. "Did he freak out?"

"Well, I wouldn't say he freaked out. He made it clear that he wasn't going to stop his attempts to develop his own prototype. To sell to his buyer with or without me." The first trace of regret appeared on his face, in the frown lines around his mouth. They were etched much deeper now than I remember them ever being.

Grace clicked her tongue. "So what does this all mean for us, then?" she asked. "He's got a buyer, but we've got the prototype with us. He can't do anything as long as we've got it."

"That's not exactly correct," Dad said. "We've got my ring, but Nolan's made one of his own. And he's dangerously close to perfecting his technology. I've seen his research. He has all the pieces. He ambushed you on the ship to steal mine."

"Why would he need yours if he's already got one?" I asked.

Dad tilted his head. "If you had a ring worth billions,

would you want someone running around with the same thing?"

"He wants to wipe out his competition." Leo let his chin fall into the palm of his hand.

Dad nodded. "At any cost, yes. As long as my prototype exists, Nolan knows his isn't worth as much money to those who want to make it a weapon. And he'll do anything to protect its value. Which is why he can't be allowed to go through with the sale. We have to get his ring before it's too late."

"Wait." I held up my hand. "You want us to steal *his* ring? We're supposed to be thinking about Mary here."

To my surprise, it was Grace who answered. "We can't leave it there, Tesla. Would you want that sort of power to be available to anyone with enough cash? Because Mike's right. Whoever this Nolan fellow wants to sell the ring to? They are *definitely* evil. Think of what they could do with it! It's our job. We can do both—we can save Mary and steal the ring—if we're smart about it."

My thoughts buzzed in circles. We'd been kept in the dark so much throughout this mission, hearing Dad's side of things was like seeing light for the first time. There were so many layers to this story that we hadn't known.

That is, if they were *true*.

Leo sighed. "If this guy is what you say he is, he's got

to have a state-of-the-art security system in place. He must be shrouded behind miles of protection."

Dad nodded. "His research is highly classified, yes. And his lab is protected by the best security systems known to man."

"How are you planning on breaking in, then?" Grace asked.

A mischievous smile grew on Dad's face. "I already have."

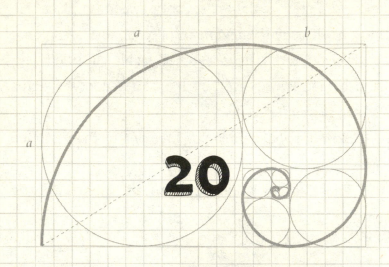

20

Bert narrowed his eyes. "*Er*... not to be rude, but... are you sure? There have been a lot of developments in cybersecurity in the past several years. Is it possible he's planted a false trail for you?"

I bit back my grin. Someone calling my dad old shouldn't have been the high point of my day, but it totally was.

"Is that so?" Dad's eyebrows lifted. "Mind handing me that laptop of yours?"

Too baffled to argue, Bert reached over and handed him the laptop. Dad opened it and immediately, his fingers began flying over the keys.

"Genius Academy has impressive security for its student database, correct?"

Bert puffed up his chest. "Of course," he answered. "One of the toughest systems in the world. I designed it myself, with Leo and three of the world's top cybersecurity agents."

Dad didn't answer, and a dark cloud of concentration settled over his face, like he was having a secret conversation with the screen. Then, a few seconds later, he looked up.

"Albert Einstein," Dad read aloud. He turned the screen to give us a better view. The Academy logo was displayed at the top. "No middle name. Son of Hermann Einstein. Twelve years old. Joined Genius Academy after several unsuccessful attempts at public elementary school and an incident that involved hacking into the school's bank accounts to purchase forty thousand snack-sized chocolate bars for the vending machines. Favorite color: blue. Childhood best friend: Schnookums." Dad tilted his head to inspect the picture on the screen. "Who is apparently a stuffed bird. A penguin, is it?" His eyes twinkled.

Schnookums

Bert's face blanched. "P-puffin," he croaked. "Schnookums was a puffin. That's *classified*." His voice cracked on the word.

"Whoa," breathed Mo, inspecting the screen.

Dad smiled, giving me the tiniest of winks. "Do I need to have thirty pizzas delivered to your parents' house for me to prove my point?"

At his words, the inner war I'd been having started to erupt again. My emotions and logic could not find common ground. I knew how I *should* feel about Dad. No matter how brilliant he was or how cool his invention had turned out to be, he was still someone who had nearly killed a bunch of innocent people with a *bomb*. That fact kept pecking at my mind like a rabid chicken, and nothing he did or said now would take that away.

But . . . a strange, traitorous sense of pride still swelled inside of me as I watched him. My father was a mystery to me, but he was also *easily* the smartest person I'd ever encountered. Responsible for the single most amazing piece of technology that our universe had ever known. The fact that *my* dad had invented such a thing made a bizarre tendril of admiration grow inside me.

And I hated it.

Can you separate what someone creates from who they are as a person? What if the parts of me that were like Dad—my love of science and inventing things—somehow came paired with the awful parts of him? I desperately wanted to ask Dad a zillion more questions. But another part of me wanted to never speak to him again, to shut him out for good and pretend he never even existed.

What do you do when you're so conflicted?

Dad snapped the computer shut. "Now hopefully you'll take me seriously. I know a threat when I see one. I just didn't realize Nolan would take things as far as he did. I never meant to put any of you in danger . . ." His lip curled in anger. "As to how I got the footage of your friend, Nolan isn't one for a change in routine. He's remained in the same laboratory since the early days. He basically inherited all my equipment after I . . ."

"After you *died*," I said pointedly, filling in the blank for him.

"Yes," he said. "But thankfully, I put appropriate measures in place as soon as I suspected he was sneaking around. Video, tracking, the works. I've got the whole laboratory wired."

Mo cleared his throat loudly and held up his hand. "I've got a question." His mouth was drawn in a thin line. "How *exactly* did you test the ring's functionality? Isn't it kind of . . . dangerous? You must have had to use this thing on yourself, right? Or . . . ?" His glance flicked nervously to Leo.

Images of the monsters in his folders flashed back in my mind. I hadn't thought of that.

A muscle in Dad's jaw jumped, and his upbeat smile had vanished.

"I did," he admitted. "Once I realized that the ring uses human emotions and intentions to work, I needed a human subject. I couldn't exactly ask someone else to do it for me. That wouldn't be right, especially without knowing any of the risks. I had a few close calls, but it didn't take me long to master the transitions."

I let out a tiny breath of relief. At least no one else had been subjected to dangerous trials.

"And how do emotions fit in?" Leo asked, leaning closer.

"The ring has a type of cellular memory, and heightened emotions seem to hasten its ability to transform its wearer."

"Wait, are you saying that ring *knows* you?" Mo asked, tilting his head in confusion.

Dad considered this. "In its own way, yes. It's no different from a personalized app on your phone," he said. "It remembers our experiences together. The more emotion I put behind it and the clearer my intention, the better the result will be."

"Do you think you could control the ring if you weren't wearing it?" Grace asked.

"I've actually never had a chance to try that out." Dad looked sheepish. "It's always been just me with this ring. And there's no way I would test that on anyone."

"Wow." Even Grace was impressed, while the realization that Dad was some super genius who had chosen to test this ring on himself made my thoughts even murkier. Another mystery surfaced as I listened to him: If he was so smart, how did he manage to accidentally blow up his lab all those years ago? And how come he couldn't manage to send me and my mom a letter to let us know he was alive? Why wait seven years to reach out?

The equation didn't make sense. He had to be keeping something from us.

From *me*.

"So we break in, get Mary, steal Nolan's prototype, and get out. Is that it?" I sighed deeply, letting the last of my resolve against Dad's plan drain away. Logically, I knew Grace and the others were right. We couldn't just leave Nolan's ring in dangerous hands. But in my heart? Nothing was nearly so clear.

Dad ran a shaky hand through his messy hair. "I've got a plan. We'll each have a role to play, but I think we can succeed if we all work together. So what do you say? Are you in?"

I didn't need to be a genius to see that the others were already on board, nodding in eager agreement. They believed every word he said, which made me realize something I hadn't wanted to face. Sometimes, no matter how many times you try to tweak the variables, an experiment fails, and you've got to deal with the disappointment. My dad might have fooled my friends, but I was only going along with his plan because getting Mary home was my top priority.

It was official.

We were going to break into a top-secret laboratory and steal a ring that could turn everyday people into monstrous killing machines. And my potentially dangerous, *definitely* criminal, genius absentee father was going to help us do it.

What could go wrong?

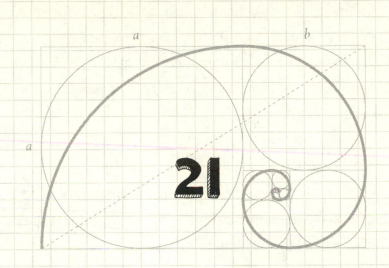

I am a strong, capable person who isn't afraid of heights.
I am a strong, capable person who isn't afraid of heights.

Has anyone ever told you that using a positive mantra can help boost your self-confidence and ability to get through difficult situations? I bet they have. People *love* to spout that stuff.

If you want my opinion, those people are *liars*. My mantra was giving me zero self-confidence, and so far, thousands of feet in the air, the only thing I'd gained was a serious case of the jitters and acid reflux. Because guess what: The grand plan of my father's to break into Nolan's lab? The one that we'd all agreed to, because we are absolutely insane? He'd neglected to mention one very crucial detail: Because of Nolan's security systems, we would have to *parachute* in, land on the top of the building in the dead of night, and break in from the roof.

Yeah, you read that right.

Parachute.

As in, fly thousands of feet in the air, jump out of a plane, and hopefully avoid falling to our deaths and splattering into a huge ugly mess.

Jump. Out of a plane. On *purpose.*

Trust me, I'm as thrilled about all of that as I sound. Flying a plane? I could handle that. But *leaping out of one*?

Barf.

What if our parachutes didn't open? What if Dad was truly and completely bananas and couldn't be trusted to get us down safely? What if we were struck by lightning and lost consciousness before our chutes deployed?!

Nobody else seemed to be worried. In fact, they were downright eager to jump. Bunch of maniacs, I say.

"Whose bright idea was it to have a ton of Mexican food before this mission?" I whined, unable to stop staring out the window into the darkness below. I tried to imagine that I was still planted firmly on the ground, rather than hovering at roughly fifteen thousand feet and about to jump to my doom.

Grace grabbed me by the shoulders and gave me a hard stare. "You'll be fine, Tesla," she affirmed. "Know what the hardest thing about skydiving is?"

I swallowed down my almost-barf and blinked at her, desperate for all the help I could get. "What?"

She clapped her hand once against my elbow with a grin. "The ground."

"Oh, *real* nice, wise leader!" I wailed, ignoring Charlie's laughter from the other side of the plane.

"Don't worry," Dad said, giving me a small smile. "You'll go tandem with me. You won't even have to pull the cord. I'll get you there safely."

Ugh. *Don't remind me,* I thought. Skydiving was one thing, but trusting *Dad* of all people to get me down safely? How come I was the only genius of the group who didn't know how to skydive? You know that feeling, when a train is approaching, and you can sense the rumbling begin under your feet?

That's what waiting for this mission to begin was to me: a charging train.

And there was no way to get off the tracks.

"We're all set!" Grace walked down our lineup and checked the oxygen. "You know the drill. Deploy your chutes when the guidance system says to. Not before. Not after. We'll meet on Nolan's rooftop."

Everyone nodded and began to file toward the open door, hanging on to a network of bars above our heads to keep balanced.

"Right now?" My hands began to shake uncontrollably. "We can't circle a little longer?" The desperation was thick in my voice. "You guys go ahead." I urged them forward with my hands. "We'll meet you there."

Leo grabbed both of my hands in his. "I'll see you down there," he confirmed, giving my palms a squeeze. "It's all going to be okay."

"You'll take care of Pickles, right?" The back of my throat ached with sadness. Because I'd be jumping with Dad, there was no safe way to secure Pickles to our suits, so Leo was taking on the task of getting her down safely with him. The poor thing had *no* idea what she was getting into, but I reasoned that it was probably best that way. Could ferrets be afraid of heights?

Too late to consider that now.

"Of course." He patted his upper shoulder, where Pickles was strapped in, complete with her own tiny set of eye goggles for protection.

I fidgeted with the GeckoDot on the collar of my flight suit, desperate for something to do with my nervous hands. "I'll see you soon. No dying, okay?"

I had to bite back a scream at the sight of my friends leaping out of the plane one by one, their arms outstretched like birds in black jumpsuits. They didn't even hesitate. Meanwhile, I was about ten seconds away from losing my cookies, and I hadn't even taken the big plunge yet!

Just before her jump, Grace gave me a thumbs-up, and I had to grip the bar above my head extra tightly to keep from yanking her away from the open door.

A few seconds after she'd gone, Dad checked the latched metal links connecting us. "Our turn, kiddo."

And that, right there—watching his boots shift on the airplane floor—*that's* when the dam inside me broke.

"I can't," I blurted out. Staring down at the inky, cloudy abyss below us was too much. My vision tunneled and I came dangerously close to passing out. "I can't do this. I know I can't."

"Sure you can, Nikki," Dad said. "You can do anything."

I shook my head, and sharp pains began to pound in my skull. "No, I can't," I said. "Not like this. Literally strapped to you. The gravity is scary enough, but I don't *trust* you, Dad! How am I supposed to jump out of a plane with you?"

I undid the clasps that connected us and tried to force deep breaths into my lungs. The others were probably opening their parachutes by now. Mary was waiting for us. We hadn't slipped the ring from Nolan's dangerous grasp. I needed to get moving or risk everything.

But fear cemented my feet to the floor of the plane. For a moment, the only sound was the whir of the engines as we shifted in the air, circling back over the drop zone.

"Nikki, listen," Dad said. His face became distant, like he was looking past me. "The night I left you and your mother was the worst night of my life."

"It wasn't a great night for us either," I snapped. Instantly, images from the past bombarded me. "Things got so bad, Dad. Reporters constantly chased us down. We had to move more than a dozen times to get away from the rumors of what you had done. Kids in school bullied me so much that I had to get tutors at home. And even they never lasted long, because everyone was afraid I would turn into you. But you know all this, right? You've been spying on me for years instead of actually being my dad."

Bitterness poured out of me, red-hot like lava.

Dad hung his head. "I'm sorry, Nikki. I've gone over things in my head a million times, but I can never imagine an outcome that would have left us together."

"Because your lab blew up," I said.

Dad's mouth curved into a sad smile. "Nolan wanted

my technology for himself. And when he proposed that we work together and sell my ring for a fortune, he wouldn't take no for an answer."

I listened, curious why Dad was bringing up Nolan again.

"The night I left you, Nolan had stopped by the house. He had the ring with him." Beads of sweat began to glisten on Dad's forehead. "I don't know how he got it, or why he even let on that he had it. You were playing with the new microscope your mother and I had gotten you earlier. Do you remember the one? With the red plastic slide and blue eyepieces? You loved that thing."

My memory flashed back. I couldn't recall Dr. Nolan's visit, but I did remember that microscope. Mom had cut up onion membranes super thin so I could examine them. I even yanked out strands of my own hair to see what they looked like under the lens.

Placing Dad alongside those memories was like trying to force a puzzle piece that didn't quite fit.

"So I was there when he came to see you?" I asked. Prickles of fear popped up on my arms and the back of my neck, mingling with the frigid high-altitude air.

"You were." His face blanched at the memory. "In fact, he was already at the house when I got home

from work. You had the ring in your hands when I walked in."

"*What?*" My mouth dropped open. "He gave something that dangerous to a little kid? I could have— That's horrible!"

A bitter shard of pain cracked Dad's expression. "I will never forget the look on your face when I leaped forward to snatch it from your hands. But before I could get my hands on it, Nolan blocked my way."

I had to sit down. Leaning my back against the shaking wall of the plane, I couldn't believe what I was hearing. What if I'd changed myself into a mermaid? Or a spider? Kids wanted to be stupid stuff all the time—what if I'd actually *done* it? I would have never understood how to get back to myself.

Suddenly, Dad's invention didn't feel like a treasure. It felt like a curse. Like something that must be destroyed at all costs.

"Why would Nolan do such a thing?" I was afraid to know the answer.

"It was a threat," he said. "Nolan was convinced that my family kept me from reaching my potential. He watched me taking time away from work to be with you and saw it as a weakness. So he used the only leverage he could think of to get me to go along with his plans. That's when I knew I had to take drastic measures to protect you and your mother."

"So what did he do next?"

"He knew that I could ruin his attempts to make his billions with the ring. You can't have competitors who know your secrets. If I wasn't on his side, I was against him. And to him, that meant I was an enemy he had to destroy. And he almost did."

The truth hit me all at once. "Your laboratory," I gasped.

"You guessed it. If you can't beat 'em, blow 'em up. That's Nolan's philosophy. He planted a bomb in my laboratory that was set to explode when he knew I would be there."

"Why weren't you?" I stopped myself. That didn't sound right. "I didn't mean it like that."

"It was show-and-tell day in your kindergarten class," he said. "You wanted to show off your latest invention: an automatic mane dryer for your unicorn dolls."

"The *Mane-o-Matic*?" I shouted. "I remember that now! It had a special setting for glitter manes, and one for . . ." I snapped my fingers, trying to recall the details. "Um, um . . ."

"A hoof shiner that made them sparkle like *diamonds*," Dad finished for me, grinning.

Instantly, I remembered not only the invention, but the embarrassing jingle I'd created to go with it. God, I was such a nerd, even back then.

"You remember all that?" I blinked at him.

Mane-o-
Matic

"Of course I do, Nikki," he said. "You're my daughter. I remember everything. I sure wasn't going to miss your first official invention reveal. And that's where Nolan made his mistake."

"He thought you'd be at your lab instead," I guessed.

"It didn't even occur to him that I would miss out on important work to celebrate my kid's unicorn invention. That was the fatal flaw in his plan. He underestimated how much I love you."

"So you didn't blow up your lab."

It wasn't a question. I had to say it out loud. To see how it felt in my mouth. For as long as I could recall, the only truth I'd ever known was that my dad had blown up his lab. Finding out that it was all a lie shifted my whole world on its axis. Dad was giving me a whole new set of variables for the equation of my life.

He stuck his hands in the pockets of his flight suit and let his legs loll out in front of him, relaxed. "Please," he said. "Do I seem like the kind of guy who would *accidentally* blow up a lab? I've made a lot of mistakes, especially with you. But science? That's something that I can trust."

A lump formed in my throat. I knew exactly what he

meant. People were hard. Science was always easier to sort out.

But a small detail surfaced in my mind. One last thing that didn't add up.

"What about the television?" I said. "The police found those horrible plans of yours. I've got dozens of newspaper articles that reported you were going to use an explosive to hurt innocent people. But if you didn't blow the lab up, then . . ." The facts settled into place. "Nolan planted the evidence, didn't he?"

"He did," Dad said. "When he discovered I wasn't at the lab, he made it look like I was a criminal. It was a pretty effective way to keep me out of the picture."

Memories swam in front of me. "The news played out for weeks," I said. "I can remember every detail, especially Mom's expression when the reporters called you a terrorist."

He winced at the awful word. "That's when I knew. I had to leave you both to protect you. Nolan would never have left you alone if I hadn't. I told myself I would never return until I'd made it safe for you again. I made that promise, Nikki, and I don't mean to break it. And today, I need your help to keep it."

He stood up and faced the open door of the plane. The dark gray clouds that surrounded us mirrored his stormy expression. "*That's* what I wanted you to know, Nikki," he said. "For seven years, I've wanted to reach out to you and your mother. I've missed so much. But with Nolan willing to hurt you if I showed my face again, I couldn't risk it. I had to stay away for your own protection."

"So why come back now?" I gripped the overhead handle to keep my balance.

He poked the front pocket of my flight suit, where I'd stored the ring.

"When I discovered how close Nolan was to perfecting his technology, I knew it was time to take a chance. I needed help and had no one else to turn to. I never thought that the two of us would be working together like this. But I'm glad you know the truth, finally."

I took a deep breath, then reached up and connected the four clasps to secure us together. I was ready to jump, and though the night sky was still terrifying, for once I wasn't afraid of the landing. I finally had solid footing.

"I'm glad you found me, Dad," I said. "But you're wrong about one thing."

I thought of my friends, who were brave enough to explore foreign caves, steal ships, and trust a man they'd never met before. They were probably waiting for us right now, peering up into the sky from the top of Nolan's laboratory.

"What's that?" he asked.

I grinned. "It's not just the two of us."

Then I pushed him out of the airplane and into the night.

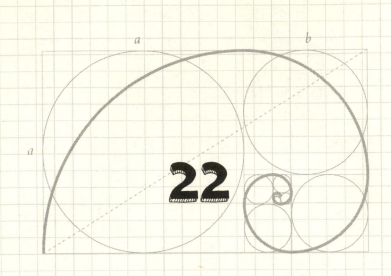

22

Let the record show that I, Nikola Tesla, did not pee my pants while skydiving.

I may have nearly puked. And I may have screamed like a little baby for the first twenty seconds of freefall. But overall, I think I handled the whole leaping-to-my-death thing pretty darn well.

Dad's landing was perfect. Our midnight black parachute was nearly invisible in the sky as we landed on the rooftop helipad. We quickly unclipped it, letting it billow away from the rooftop of Nolan's laboratory, which was nestled on a nearly empty country road far from prying eyes. The others were safely waiting for us, and there was no sign that anyone inside the building had noticed yet.

"You made it," Leo said, giving my hand a squeeze. "We heard everything, by the way." He tapped the GeckoDot on his shoulder. I'd totally forgotten that every team member had one tonight.

"Oh, *oops*." My face flushed, but I was glad I didn't have to repeat what I'd learned from Dad on the plane. It was time to move forward, not backward.

Leo turned to Dad. "I knew you were a good guy, Mike."

"Is everyone ready?" Charlie cracked her knuckles. "This highly secure laboratory isn't going to break into itself."

"Wait," Mo hissed, cupping his hand to his ear. He stepped closer to the edge of the roof, listening intently. "Do you hear that?"

I wiped a trickle of sweat from my forehead and tried to focus on the sounds around me. Cicadas trilled in the air, but I couldn't detect anything out of the ordinary.

"What is it?" Leo strained to listen to the dark.

Mo narrowed his eyes into the distance. "It's the whoop of a siren," he said. "Miles away but headed this direction."

Dad scrunched his nose. "Are you sure? Because I can't hear a thing . . ."

"If it's making a sound, Mo can hear it," Leo said, rocking back on his heels. "Maybe the police?"

"Bert." Grace lifted her nose, as though she was sniffing the air. Sniffing out trouble. "Got your radio on you? Can you dial into the local police frequencies? I have a bad feeling about this."

Bert pulled a small handheld signaler from his pocket and held it to his ear as a flash of purple in the distance caught my eye.

"There," I said, pointing at the lights. "Blue and red lights."

"Drat!" Charlie said. "The cavalry's coming."

Bert's face fell as he held out the signaler to Grace. "They're on their way, all right," he explained. "I'm afraid you're not dead anymore, Mike."

"What?" I gawked at him.

"To the authorities," Bert clarified. "Nolan must have tipped them off. Your dad is all over their radio waves. They're looking for him so they can arrest him for his past crimes."

"Crimes!" I spat. "He was framed!"

"They don't know that," Bert sighed.

"So what do we do?" I asked.

A sharp pang of worry shot through me. I didn't know what kind of relationship I would have with my dad after seven years apart, but the thought of losing him made me feel sicker than skydiving. I wanted time to sort out what he was to me now.

I looked to Grace for her opinion. "Can we leave him here on the roof while we go get Mary and Nolan's prototype?"

Grace opened her mouth to speak, but Dad interrupted her. "Not a chance," he said, shaking his head. "I'm going with you. We all have jobs, remember? You'll need help once we get inside, and I'm not letting you anywhere near Nolan on your own, Nikki." He looked around the group. "*None* of you will be alone with him. Is that understood?"

Grace gave him a lopsided grin. "So what about the police?"

Dad scanned the roof, his gaze coming to rest on Bert. "What if we had some backup?" he asked.

"What did you have in mind?" Bert cocked his head. "A diversion?"

Dad clicked his tongue. "That research we were chatting about earlier . . . Do you have any working prototypes?"

A glimmer of intrigue spread over Bert's face.

Prototypes? I hadn't heard anything about Bert's latest research, but somehow Dad had?

"What research?" Grace put her hand on her hip. "You holding out on us, Albert?"

Bert shuffled his feet. "No!" he said. "It's just some new technology I was developing . . . Something I've been doing for fun."

"Explosives," Dad said, making no attempt to hide his smirk. "Bert here has developed a pretty revolutionary concept that can be made with minimal ingredients. It's completely unlike any explosive on the market today. They also create a nonviolent light show that might come in handy in a pinch."

"So . . . fireworks?" I tried not to look unimpressed, but considering Bert was one of the greatest minds on the planet, I expected a bit more than a glorified Fourth of July celebration.

Bert bit his lip, and his chest puffed up with pride. "Like fireworks," he said. "But much smaller, with a bigger bang. And they're compact. Thinner than a sheet of paper. Of course I brought some. I've been waiting for the perfect time to test them out."

"Well, buddy, I'd say tonight's your lucky night." Leo clapped him on the back. "We can use that. Grace, Nikki, Charlie, Mo, and I will storm the castle, deal with Mary, and find Nolan's research. You can be on police patrol. Your job is to distract the cops looking for Mike. Keep them occupied as far away from the lab as you can."

Bert drummed his fingernails against his leg. "And how am I supposed to get down to the ground, huh?" he asked. He glanced over the edge of the roof nervously.

Grace nudged him toward the pile of black parachute material that lay balled up by his feet. "You're a genius," she said. "I'm sure you'll figure it out."

Bert's shoulders drooped. "*Fine.* Charlie, can you help secure this thing, please? Maybe we can use it to lower me down . . ." The two of them began hauling the parachute material to the east side of the roof.

Before the rest of us could get in position, Dad grabbed my hand. "Nikki," he said, his voice hushed, "one more thing. Leo, Grace, Mo, I want you to hear this, too. If things get out of control inside, promise me that you and the others will clear out."

191

I scoffed. "Dad, please. I'm not going to leave you there alone. Don't forget that Mary is in there because of *me*. I'm doing everything I can to get her out safely."

Dad's jaw clenched. "I'll appeal to your intelligence, then. You're all smart. If you calculate—if you *know*—that the chances of winning this fight are zilch, promise me you'll all get out of here. How does that sound? We have a deal?"

I considered this. If I *truly* thought the situation was hopeless, would I want to stay and fight? It seemed to me that living to fight another day was always the smartest option. Dad wasn't asking me to leave when *he* said it was time. He was leaving it up to me to decide.

I could handle that.

I glanced at Grace, who nodded once.

"Deal," I said.

Dad's shoulders dropped in relief.

Leo grinned. "Glad we got that covered," he said. "We should probably make sure that Bert doesn't topple off this building."

"Thanks, Leo," I said. Suddenly, I was super aware of my dad watching us. I cleared my throat and pretended to adjust my GeckoDot.

Grace and Charlie trotted up beside us. "Bert made it safely to the ground. Operation Distraction is a go.

Everyone, check your GeckoDots. We can't risk any mis-communications tonight."

I pulled the dot from my collar and gave it a tap. If only we'd been able to sneak one of these on Mary, we could let her know we hadn't left her behind. I squeezed my eyes shut, willing her to stay safe and unharmed.

Dad pointed to the duo of police cars making their way up the long stretch of road to Nolan's laboratory. "I sure hope Bert knows what he's doing."

"Wait for it." Grace squinted at the distance. "Any second now . . ."

A bright flash erupted on the ground below us, accompanied by a shattering bang. It was quickly followed by a sharp hoot of excitement from Bert.

The plan was in motion . . . whether we were ready or not.

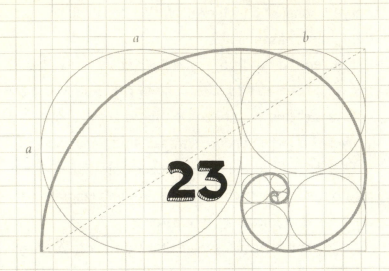

23

If you ever need to create a diversion, I highly recommend you borrow a genius. Bert did his job, all right—a funnel of blue smoke spiraled through the air like a rogue balloon deflating. The police skidded to a stop a couple hundred yards away from us, gawking at the display.

And what a display it was. We spotted Bert driving a hot pink van, which jerked its way up the road, sending off sprays of sonic fireworks in random bursts out its open rear door. The words "You Look Fetching" were spray-painted across the side, along with some cartoon pictures of shaggy dogs.

"Did he *find* a mobile dog-washing van?" Dad asked. "Or did he make one?"

"Bert's very creative," Charlie said. "And great at hot-wiring. Plus, he's probably been carrying that spray paint for weeks, waiting for the perfect opportunity to use it."

I watched in amusement as the police ducked behind their cars and fanned away the harmless smoke. Eventually, the fireworks stopped, and the pink van careened down the road. Immediately, the officers hopped back in their cruisers and sped after him. They couldn't let a menace like Bert Einstein wreak havoc on public streets! And Bert knew it. He took a right turn at the corner, leading the police far from the target of our mission.

"And away they go," I said. As long as they stayed away for a while, Dad wouldn't need to worry about getting recognized or arrested.

"Time for part two," Grace said. "The moment we've all been waiting for. Charlie, are you sure about this?"

Our plan was simple. We'd parachuted onto the sub-roof, but according to Dad's schematics, the only way into the compound that was out of range of video surveillance was an upper window in the northeast corner. It was seven floors above us, and without a net to catch us if we slipped, Grace decided it was far too dangerous to climb, even with my Gecko Gloves.

That's where Dad's ring came in.

Someone needed to get up there.

No. *Fly* up there.

Charlie grabbed the ring from my open palm. "You bet I am! Charlotte Darwin, to the rescue!" She stuck the ring on her pointer finger and held her chin high. "I'll fly up there and break in through the ventilation duct like we discussed. Then I'll sabotage the cameras on these windows here, and Bob's your uncle, in you go."

I grabbed her arm. "Be careful, okay?" I asked. "This is serious. You'll need to be a *bird*."

"That's the best part." She beamed. "I can handle a little pain. I've always wanted to be a bird, and when else am I going to get the chance?" She cocked her head and tossed her ponytail over her shoulder. "What *species* should I be, hmm?" She gazed into the distance, getting lost in her thoughts. "Don't want to be a penguin or ostrich now, do I? That won't come in handy at all. Ooh, maybe I should be one of those lovely little finches from the Galápagos!"

"Charlie!" I shook her arm. "Focus! Pick any bird that is small enough to go unnoticed but able to fly all the way up there." I pointed to the top of the building.

"That's right," Dad confirmed. "You want to blend in, not stand out. Good luck, Charlie. Remember what we practiced. You need to *feel* it in your bones. Mind over matter."

"Mind over matter. Bird over girl. Don't worry, guys. I got this. I'll be five, six minutes, tops." She cleared her throat and blinked up at the height. "Maybe seven, if I take a joy ride first."

"*Charlie*," Grace warned.

"Okay, okay. Not the time for laughs." She gave me a quick hug and saluted everyone.

"Good luck, Chuck," Leo added.

Charlie stepped to the edge of the building and turned her back to us.

"I can't do this if you're all staring at me!" Charlie said, swiveling around. "It's like peeing when someone's listening to you!"

Grace laughed. "We'll turn around," she said. She gestured for us to do the same.

I bit my fingernails and counted the seconds. Amazingly, only a few had passed before Grace spoke again. "She's done it! Wow, look at that." She craned her neck to squint up at a faint flicker of reflected moonlight on gray feathers.

The pride on Dad's face was clear. "That was an incredibly seamless transformation."

"That's Charlie for you," Mo said. "If anyone was going to be good at becoming an animal, it was her."

"Now what?" I asked.

Grace crossed her arms and focused on the inky darkness. "Now we wait for a little bird to let us in."

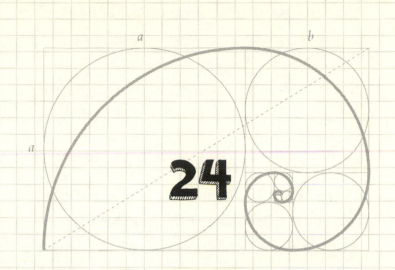

24

It seemed like even the trees around us were holding their breath, and the wind settled into silence as we waited for Charlie to safely make it inside. If you've ever wondered what it feels like to be stranded on a rooftop while a bird holds your fate in its mischievous British wings, it feels a lot like trying to sneak into your house when you're late for curfew and you know your mom will flip if she sees that you're not in your pajamas yet.

Of course, in my case, I was only ever late for curfew because I was out testing one of my inventions or trying to sneak into a local electronics store to steal—no, *borrow*—some tools.

I guess some things don't change.

Mo was right: Charlie was a natural at being a bird, because four minutes later, we heard her voice whispering out of all our GeckoDots.

"I'm in," she said. Her words sounded tight, like she was caught in a small space without enough air. "The window should be open now."

"Charlie!" Grace said. "You're okay? Did anyone see you?" The muscles in her neck strained as she tilted her ear closer to the GeckoDot on her shoulder.

A beam of light shot from my dot. Charlie, broadcasting her location for us. "Of course nobody saw me!" she said. "I'm a ghost, I tell you. But *look.*"

The image flickered in and out of focus. Glass walls, sterilized white counters, and metal lab stools were everywhere. Charlie was somehow moving *above* each room, and the video display focused on her bird's-eye view of the space.

"Charlie, what are you?" My curiosity got the best of me.

"'*Where* am I' would be a better question," she answered. "See for yourself."

She stopped moving and the image focused below again, revealing the white-tiled room below. Right in the middle, alone and silent, sat a very disheveled-looking girl in a chair.

"It's Mary!" Leo gasped. His feet began to shift automatically on the hard concrete roof, eager to get moving.

Grace examined the image in front of us. "So where are you exactly? The rest of us can come help you free Mary while Nikki and her dad find Nolan's prototype."

"There's no time," Charlie responded. "I'm in the overhead ducts. She's unguarded right now. I have to save her! I can drop down directly into her room. The two of us will be able to find a way out together, I know it. You guys can deal with the research and Nolan's prototype. Trust me, Grace. We have to adapt here. This opportunity is too good to pass up. I can get Mary out!"

Grace frowned. I knew how much she hated to stray from her plans. Nothing Grace did was haphazard, and there was always a strategy behind everything. But she was also quick on her feet and recognized a lucky break when she saw one.

"Are you positive that she's unguarded? Can you wait for one of us to come and help? I don't want you doing this on your own, Charlie. We can take the same route you did once we're inside."

Charlie giggled. "That's going to be a bit of a pickle, my friend. The ducts are small. Like…" She paused. "*Mouse* small."

My jaw dropped. "Did you turn into a mouse?!"

Leo cackled over my shoulder. "Told you she'd be good at this."

"Maybe," Charlie said. The image shifted down to Charlie's feet. Or, rather, her *paws*. They were tiny and white, with small pink toes and sharp claws.

Ever since I first met Charlie, I'd always thought she was incredibly mouselike. Squeaky, high-pitched voice. Darting eyes. Slight frame. I shouldn't have been surprised, really.

"And you didn't find it difficult to transform more than once in such a short time frame?" Dad asked. He blinked in awe at the toes projected in the air in front of me.

"Nah," Charlie said. "Clear your head and think like an animal, right? That's what you said. I can do that."

"Charlie, that's brilliant," Grace said. "Okay. If we can't get to you, then as you say, we'll have to adapt. You and Mary escape however you can. With the windows unsecured and nobody guarding her, you should be okay." Concern clouded Grace's face. I could practically see the gears turning as she weighed every option. "But if you need any help once you two get moving, call us. You hear me? Once we're inside, I'm going to send Pickles after you—tie the ring to her collar. We may need it once you two are out of there." She glanced at me with a pained expression.

"I promise," Charlie said. "I'll let you know when we're home free."

We watched with awe as Charlie squeezed her way under the mesh duct in the ceiling. Below her, Mary sat upright in a chair. Her hair was a bit frizzy and her shirt was creased and dirty, but she seemed otherwise unharmed. She wasn't even tied up, which meant that Nolan was either incredibly stupid or the door to the room was locked from the inside. Everyone underestimated Mary.

I covered my dot and whispered to Grace, "What if they can't get out?" I pointed to the door. "That's got to be locked."

Grace grinned. "Charlie's our best escape artist. And that's when she doesn't have a ring to make her the size of a mouse. They'll be fine."

I hoped Grace was right. Charlie crept closer until she hung almost directly above Mary. She could drop right into her lap if she wanted to.

"Psst!" Charlie whispered.

"She's going to scare the pants off Mary!" Mo giggled.

Mary looked up, and a burst of warmth shot through

me. I wanted to reach out and hug her right there. Ever since joining Genius Academy, I'd been grateful to have her as a best friend. But it's only when you lose someone that you really understand how important they are to you. Mary was like a sister to me. She was one of the big reasons I had a home now, with real friends.

"Who's there?" Mary asked. She kept her voice low, leaning slowly and deliberately away from the overhead vent. She knew something was up.

Though I bet she'd never have guessed it was Charlie in mouse form, literally *up* above her.

"I'm turning the camera off now guys," Charlie whispered. "I don't want the light to get anyone's attention."

"Go get her, buddy." Leo tightened his own jacket collar, like he was preparing to save Mary himself.

The last thing we saw was Mary's wide, shocked face at the sight of a white mouse plummeting down on top of her out of nowhere.

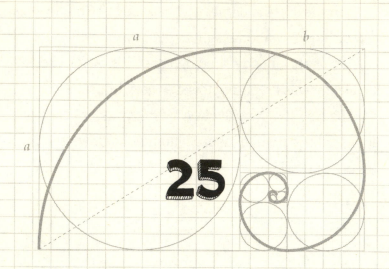

25

You want to know the most annoying thing about far-fetched, intricate plans to invade villainous laboratories? It's how many stinking obstacles you face, one right after another.

It's beyond frustrating.

With Charlie taking care of Mary, the rest of us turned our attention to part three of our plan. Getting inside the window was easy enough—Charlie had seen to that by shifting the surveillance cameras out of range for us in her bird form. But what I wasn't anticipating was the sheer number of hallways and rooms inside the compound, each crawling with scientists who might notice we didn't belong here before we could find Nolan and his research.

"I know where we are," Dad said, shifting on his feet. "This way!"

Grace, Leo, Mo, and I raced after him, doing our best to avoid making any noise on the shiny white floor. When we reached the end of a long hallway, Dad shoved a door open with his shoulder. "In here! Quick!"

I was hoping that Dad had led us straight to Nolan's workspace, where we could find his ring prototype right away. But no such luck. Instead of a pristine lab space with computers, wires, and tools, we faced a bunch of brooms, mops, buckets, and soap bottles.

"A janitor's closet?" I said. I nudged a grimy mop with the toe of my shoe. "Not exactly the high-tech environment I was picturing."

"Nolan keeps his prototype in Lab A," Dad explained. "But it's a maze in here, and I thought you should get your bearings before we split up. Nikki, you and I need to go left, right, and then left to get to Lab A. Who's next?"

"Pickles." Leo glanced at me for approval before setting her on the floor. I was fairly certain we could rely on her to find Charlie and retrieve the ring for us, but my stomach still flip-flopped at the idea of setting her loose in such a dangerous place.

"Find Charlie," I told her. I pulled one of Charlie's old socks out of my pack. I had one for each member of the team—definitely the weirdest bag of laundry ever. When Pickles found Charlie and Mary, Charlie would use the same trick to send Pickles back to us with the ring.

Pickles sniffed the sock and seemed to understand.

"My turn," Leo said. "Where are the data servers?" He patted his jacket pockets, which he'd stuffed full of explosive charges for his part of the plan: destroying Nolan's research.

Dad closed his eyes, and the tops of his eyelids fluttered as he traced a map in his head. "Right, right, left, right. Room 442. Do you have that?"

Leo nodded. "I'll keep in touch and let you know when the charges are set. Good luck, guys." He gave my hand a quick squeeze before straightening up and slinking out the door with Pickles.

Grace peered out the tiny slit in the doorway to watch him. "He's around the corner." She relayed Leo's movements so we could keep up. "Pickles took off. I think she's heading in Charlie's direction. Oh, *shoot*."

A wave of dizziness swept over me as I pulled her out of the way to see for myself. "What is it?! Did they get caught?" The image of Leo being dragged away by one of these horrible scientists made me want to scream.

"*Shh!*" Grace said. She yanked me out of sight and eased the door closed quietly. "It's the guards."

"What about them?" Mo asked. "Need me to knock someone out?" He lifted his fists. I couldn't help but giggle. Mo was all muscle and the size of a small fridge, but he was also about as physically harmless as a stuffed puffin named Schnookums.

Dad rubbed his temples with his fingers, frowning. "There shouldn't be guards here," he said. "Nolan must have changed his security layout. Are they on the left or right?" His mouth pinched into a tight line.

"There's a security station on the left," Grace said. "Sorry, Mike."

"What?" I looked between them. "What does this mean?"

"It means our plan is dead in the water," Grace said. She grimaced and shook her head angrily. "The guards are stationed right in our path. We need to go left to reach Nolan's lab."

"No." Mo poked me in the shoulder, then turned to

Grace. "*We* don't. *They* do." Taking hold of her elbow, he dragged her to the door.

"Mo!" I said. "What are you doing?! Stay in here!"

He cracked the door open and whispered, pointing to the hallway. "You'll be able to navigate to Nolan's room if you're careful. But only if the security guards aren't looking your way! Come on, Grace, we can give them cover."

To my surprise, Grace didn't argue. Instead, she lifted her hand to the air for a high five. "Excellent," she said. "You want to do Waterworks or False Alarm?"

"Wait, what?" I asked.

Mo waved his hand at me dismissively. "Don't worry, we got this. Let's go with Waterworks. Better odds in this place."

"Perfect," Grace agreed. "Wait three minutes for us to get around the corner!"

Shoving the door open, Mo and Grace stumbled out of the janitor's closet, while Dad and I stayed hidden in the darkness. They timed it perfectly. The guards turned around to find my friends standing in the middle of the hallway, as if they'd appeared out of nowhere.

"Hey!" One guard pointed at the two of them. "Who are you?"

Panic gripped me. How on earth would they talk their way out of this?

As it happened, their plan wasn't to *talk* at all.

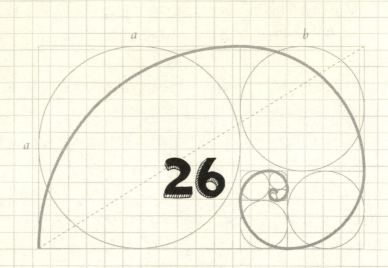

26

First Grace fell to the floor. Then Mo's high-pitched screech pierced my eardrums as it echoed through the narrow hallway. He rushed toward the security guard sat a full sprint.

"Please!" he cried. I'd never heard him sound so distraught. "My cousin! We're visiting my mom today—she's a receptionist here—and she sent us to the break room to grab some juice! But she got hurt! Look at her wrist!"

Tears of panic streamed down Mo's face as he made a show of picking up Grace's red-splotched wrist—still angry-looking from the chemical burn—and flopping it around. "I don't know what she touched, but it burned her and she passed out!"

Grace, amazingly, didn't crack a smile or giggle at Mo's antics. Instead, she let her head loll to the side while her arm flopped unceremoniously over her chest and Mo continued to shake her like a terrified teddy bear. For a moment, their acting was so good, I had to remind myself that Grace hadn't actually fainted.

"She's got low blood sugar, too!" Mo continued, panting with fear. He spoke at such a fast clip I could barely understand him. "I told her to have a cookie earlier, but she refused! She hates raisins, and I only had oatmeal raisin in my backpack! Oh, I should have known better! Why didn't I think to bring chocolate chip?! *What kind of a person only brings oatmeal raisin?!* Mom is going to lose her mind!"

"Whoa, easy there, kid." The guard panicked at the shrieking outburst. He leaned in to hiss a whisper at his colleague. "If these two somehow got into dangerous chemicals, we are toast. How could this happen?!"

He used his radio to call for assistance, but after a few more seconds of Mo's panicked whining, he gave up and cursed under his breath. "I don't know how you two got up here, but we're going to find your mother *right* now, kid."

He scooped Grace up in his arms.

Mo followed the two guards, wailing his way down

the hallway. He even threw in a couple of phlegmy snorts and hiccups to sound extra hysterical.

"Wow," Dad whispered. "That kid can *act*."

"Necessity is the mother of invention," I mused. "Even for a guy who can go all day without saying a word. I didn't know he had it in him!"

"Okay, on to the next phase," Dad said. "Are you ready to find Lab A and Nolan's prototype?"

"No," I admitted. I steeled my nerves and peeked out the doorway one last time. The guards were gone, and their empty chairs spun listlessly at the far end of the hallway to our left. "But that never stopped me before."

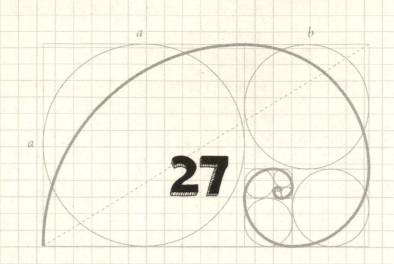

For some reason, I always assume that stepping inside the laboratory of a genius-scientist-gone-bad will be a lot like entering a villain's lair. I expect spooky music, maybe some ghost noises, sacrificial bones of fallen enemies, and all sorts of sharp objects. At the very least, I figure I'll find a rat or two.

But Dr. Nolan's laboratory wasn't scary at all. In fact, it was downright beautiful, with millions of dollars' worth of lab equipment, all sparkling with bright surfaces.

"Whoa!" I gaped in awe at the immaculate lab benches and full shelves. "It's like a spaceship in here! How could you leave?!"

Dad gave me a look.

"Right," I corrected myself. "Evil lab partner. Sorry."

Dad approached a bank of drawers. "You see these blue buttons?" he asked. "Each button opens one of the metal doors so you can see what's inside. Start pressing." He hit the button in front of him and checked his watch as he was waiting for it to slowly grind open.

A quiet mumble sounded in my ear. *Leo!*

"Hey, guys?" He sounded rushed but still all in one piece.

"Leo," I answered. "Mo and Grace can't answer— they're with the guards. But they're okay! Are you?"

"Yes!" Leo panted. "The charges are set. And guess what—Pickles already made it back to me! The ring is safe in my pocket. I'm going to come meet you guys at Nolan's laboratory, okay? I can help you look for his prototype. As soon as we find it, we can get out of here and I'll detonate my handiwork. I'm not risking any explosions while we're still in the building!"

"Sweet guy," Dad mumbled, still searching through stacks of equipment.

I envisioned Leo sneaking his way through a packed server room, surrounded by snaking wires and blinking computer lights. I shivered at the thrill of excitement. Every new mission put us in danger, but it was always such a relief when things went according to our plans. Leo had done his job. Pickles was safe.

And that also meant Charlie and Mary were on their way out.

"Okay," I said. "But be careful! Have you heard from Charlie yet?"

"I'm here!" Charlie spoke at full volume in my ear, causing me to wince at the sound.

"Ahh!" I reeled. "You're going to deafen someone!"

"Sorry," she said. The excitement in her voice was easy to read, even over the airwaves. "Mary and I are out of the building—and guess what! Martha is here! After we were out of range for so long, she found a GeckoDot at the Academy and tuned into my frequency. She flew here on the jet, and she's getting ahold of the police for us! She can explain everything to them so your dad won't be a target anymore, and get them to detain Nolan if he tries to leave! Everything's comin' up roses, I tell you!"

I beamed at Dad, who gave me a thumbs-up.

I mean, I know I've complained before about how unfair life is. But you know what? Sometimes, life hands you a win. Like when the vending machine gives you two chocolate bars instead of one. Maybe this night wasn't doomed from the beginning? Just the thought of Martha taking charge outside the building made the muscles in my shoulders unknot a tiny bit. She would know exactly what to do.

"That's amazing!" I said. "We'll be out to meet you as soon as we get Nolan's ring! Leo's ready with the explosive charges, too."

A weight on my chest lightened a tiny bit, knowing that no matter what happened next, Charlie and Mary had gotten out and would be safe.

I continued to scour each drawer with no luck. But the next button I pressed didn't open a drawer to reveal an empty white box like each of the buttons before it. Instead, it shifted to reveal a dark silver cube, clearly containing something important.

"Dad!" I whispered. "I think I found it! But it looks like we're going to need a password to get in." I tapped the side of a small metallic number pad with my fingernail. "*Tell me* you know his code!"

A satisfied smile broke out across Dad's face as he joined me. He punched in a seven-digit code, and the gears inside the cube began grinding under our hands.

"This has to be it." I ducked nervously around his arm to check the door. So far, we were still undiscovered. The faces of the cube started to lift and fall apart like the bloom of a mechanical flower, revealing a small navy blue pedestal with an etched white panel on its side.

"Prototype A," I read aloud. "But wait . . ."

My heart fell.

The cube had opened all right, but there was no ring staring back at us, just a small circular indentation on the pedestal where it would have been.

"It's gone." Dad rubbed his temples with both hands.

I bit my lip and pushed the drawer closed again, unwilling to look at its emptiness any longer.

Have you ever ridden a bike and been unable to steer because of a pothole in the road? There's that moment when your balance goes haywire, your stomach jumps to your throat, you *know* you're going to face-plant, and there's nothing you can do but lean into the fall?

That's what it felt like when we heard the man's deep voice behind us.

"Michael Faraday. It's been years, my friend."

Dad and I whirled around. My hand instinctively reached for Dad's arm. He slid forward to shield me.

Dr. Nolan looked nothing like I expected. He didn't appear worn out or disheveled like Dad. In fact, he

seemed chill. He had choppy black hair and intense eyes that scanned the room calmly like a wolf anticipating a hunt. He was very tall, and his long legs covered a lot of ground as he strode toward us. His tailored suit was unbuttoned at the neck, as though he'd been spending a late evening at work. The weirdest part was his smile— there wasn't a hint of surprise or anxiety on his face. In fact, he had the look of someone who was eager. He'd been *waiting* for us. My hands began to tremble with dread.

"Nice of you to bring your kid here," he said playfully. I couldn't believe how relaxed he sounded, like he was speaking to an old buddy instead of an enemy who was currently trying to steal his billion-dollar invention. That meant either he was totally confident he had us or he was bananas.

Or maybe even both.

He slid his dark eyes away from Dad and toward me. "Hello, Nikki."

I opened my mouth to speak, but Nolan made a face and held up his hand to shush me. He reached behind his back and calmly pulled out a small gun.

"You'd better tell those friends of yours to stay away." Dr. Nolan kept his voice low, so nobody could hear him but us. He nudged the barrel of the gun higher in the air, aiming it directly at Dad's chest. The faint sparkle of something silver on this thumb made my breath shrink down to ragged spasms.

He had the ring.

"No, please!" I whispered.

He lifted his eyebrows but didn't say another word. I couldn't decide if he was still smiling or just baring his teeth at me. I turned to Dad questioningly, and his tiny nod told me all I needed to know. We didn't have a choice.

"Leo," I whispered. "Leo, can you hear me?"

"I'm halfway to you!" he said. I could hear the gentle scuffle and slide of his sneakers on the clean floors. "Sit tight!"

"Don't come," I said, forcing my voice to be strong and clear. I had to squeeze my nails into my palm to get the words out. I wanted more than anything for Leo to come and help us—he was brave and smart, and that would mean Dad and I wouldn't have to face Nolan alone. But I would never put any of my friends in danger if I could warn them to stay away instead.

Leo would do the same for me.

"Say that again?" Leo said. "Are you telling me not to come? Nikki, what is it?"

"Y-yes," I sputtered. I swallowed down my fear and made myself stare at Dr. Nolan as I spoke, so he knew I was serious. I faked a happy, choked laugh. "Dad found the ring like he planned. It looks like Nolan has taken off already. He must have been one step ahead of us. Go meet Martha and the others outside. We'll be there as soon as we can!"

"It's true." Dad confirmed my lie. I could tell by the way his fingers reached out to mine that he wanted to squeeze my hand in support. He understood why we had to do this alone: We wouldn't risk the others for our fight. "We'll be right behind you, Leo."

I lifted my chin and raised my eyebrows at Nolan, desperate for Leo's response.

"Okay." Leo's reply was muffled but clear enough to hear. "Be careful! I'll see you outside!"

He'd believed my lie. I couldn't decide if I was happy or sad about it. Happy that Leo and the others would be able to get far away from this monster. But also sad that it meant we had no help to fight him.

We were on our own.

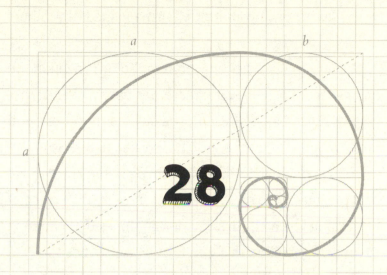

28

I plastered a mask of indifference on my face, forcing myself to think positively. Maybe if Leo and the others were safe, they could figure out a way to stop Nolan from selling the ring. It was the only hope I had left.

Facing Dr. Nolan, I gently reached up and took the GeckoDot from my collar, then reached over to do the same to Dad's. I dropped them to the floor and stepped forward, crushing them. They cracked sharply, like beetles under a boot heel.

CRUNCH

At least now, no matter what happened, the others wouldn't have to hear it.

"They're gone," I promised him. I didn't mention the charges that Leo had set. If there was even a chance that getting rid of Nolan's research would set him back and anger his buyers, even a little bit, we had to take it.

"Do you like it?" Dr. Nolan changed the subject. He held the gun out to me, like he was showing off a piece of art, or a new watch. "It's my design. Instead of shooting rudimentary bullets, this gun fires a particle beam."

I dug around for my courage, but I was fresh out. Instead, I found sarcasm. "A death ray?" I shrugged. "Big deal. I invented one, too. You're not impressing anyone. Did you put a safety on yours? You might want to. I had to, on account of my pet ferret."

Dad huffed under his breath, and he shook his head ever so slightly to catch my eye. If looks could talk, his was saying, *Stop engaging with the mad scientist.*

"Not impressed?" He aimed the gun at Dad. "How about now? For as long as I can remember, your father was never quite satisfied with my work. Do you feel that way, too, Nikki? I bet we have more in common with each other than you realize! Do you think he's proud of you?"

Nolan's hand was beginning to shake. Not great news for someone handling a deadly weapon. I was starting to realize that under his easygoing demeanor, Dr. Nolan was completely unhinged.

"I don't know," I said. "He wasn't around for most of my life. I guess that's thanks to you."

Nolan barked out a laugh. "Right!" he exclaimed. "You weren't missing much, kid. This guy is impossible to please! I bet he would keep his greatest work from you, too—he doesn't trust anyone with his designs!" His voice was almost hysterical.

"Joe, please," Dad said. "Let my daughter go, and the two of us can deal with this. There's no need to bring her into it."

Nolan shrugged. "Don't worry. I won't be hurting her. Can't say the same for you, however."

"Let her go, Joe," Dad demanded. My breath caught in my throat as he calmly began walking toward the door, dragging me with him by the arm. He was moving us closer to Nolan's death ray, convinced that he wouldn't shoot us.

But I wasn't so sure Nolan was bluffing.

"*Stop.*" Dr. Nolan's voice was a low growl.

"This is between us." Dad glanced at the door. "She doesn't know anything."

Dr. Nolan laughed. To anyone listening, he probably sounded like he was having a casual conversation.

"That's not what I heard!" he said. "If this is your kid, I bet she's a real wizard. Must take after you, Mike. Invented a *death ray* and all." His smile dropped in a flash, and he tilted his head. "Why didn't you just join me?"

He inched closer to Dad, totally ignoring me. "It's not too late, you know," Nolan continued. He was incredibly calm. How could he go from crazed to chill in 2.5 seconds? It was giving me whiplash.

"I'm not interested," Dad said.

Dr. Nolan scoffed. "Be serious, Mike," he said. "I'm selling this ring for a lot of money, and you can still have your cut. I promise you, no games. Give me your proto-type, and we'll call it even. Maybe we can even cook up some new designs together." He flashed that winning smile again. "It'd be *fun*."

"I destroyed it," Dad lied. "It's over, Joe." He kept his body angled between me and his enemy. "Your servers are fried. Your research is as good as destroyed. You kid-napped a child who attends one of the most respected government agencies in the world, and you're going to spend the rest of your life in a jail cell. Stop this now and let Nikki go."

Nolan's face dropped and, for a second, I thought he might actually surrender. It was clear by the way he looked at my dad that he respected him. Almost like he wanted to impress him, or make him proud. But under all that, rage seemed to boil away in his eyes.

"Oh yeah?" Nolan said. "We'll be long gone before the authorities get here. And as for the servers...Are you talking about the kid who set a few explosives?" He bit his lip and giggled, lifting a small memory stick between his thumb and forefinger, then tucking it into his pocket. "I've got everything I need right here."

Sweat prickled at the back of my neck. If he'd known what Leo was up to, why hadn't he stopped it? Had he *hurt* Leo? Instantly, regret began to choke me. Why had I smashed up my GeckoDot? What if my friend needed me right now?

"Relax," Nolan said. He must have been able to read the pain on my face. "I let the kid go as an act of good faith to my old lab partner. Consider it a thank-you, Mike. It was you who inspired this in the first place. You see, I can be reasonable." He lifted his hand in apology, but I could tell by the way he twisted his palm away from us he was really warning us with his ring.

Dad stepped fully in front of me, blocking Nolan. "As another act of good faith..." Dad said. "Let Nikki leave."

My feet had a mind of their own, and I began angling myself toward the door. But Dr. Nolan's cold face was

clear. Not only was he not letting me out of here, he was *enjoying* messing with us. No matter how many avenues of escape I considered, I couldn't see a way out.

"Nah," he replied. "She stays. But you're welcome to stand in front of her there if it makes you feel any better." He chuckled bitterly. "You're not *really* going to die to keep me from selling this thing, are you?" Nolan let the gun drop to his side.

Dad didn't blink. "I already died for it once."

They say that in times of extreme stress, your gut takes over. Everything slows down, and single seconds feel like hours. Maybe that's true, maybe it's not; I'm not sure. But when Nolan lifted the gun ever so slightly and narrowed his eyes at my dad, I knew without a doubt that he was about to shoot. There was nothing more to say. If I didn't act, Dad was going to die.

My gut didn't take over.

But my feet did.

I leaped forward through the air, grabbing my dad's shoulder with all my might and yanking him out of the way. Desperate to save Dad from the deadly beam, I flung myself at Dr. Nolan with a loud scream.

But I was too slow.

Thankfully, Leo wasn't.

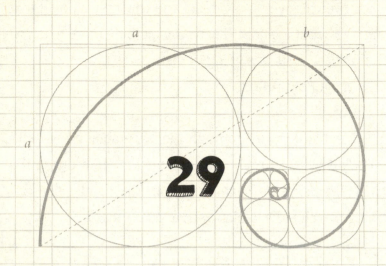

29

"Get down!" Leo flew over the top of a lab bench while simultaneously throwing something at Nolan's face. Chaotic flashes and eardrum-piercing pops filled the room as Bert's handiwork sparked a flurry of lights and thick smoke. Pickles, who must have snuck in with Leo, raced toward me across the slippery floor.

The distraction was enough to shift Nolan's aim and send his weapon clattering to the floor, where it ultimately landed under a row of shelving. When he saw that his enemy was still standing, he shoved Leo into the wall and launched himself at Dad in a fit of anger. But Dad saw it coming and lowered his shoulder to take the hit.

Nolan tackled him like a linebacker, and soon the two

of them were an angry heap of swinging arms and spit-ting curses. My hand whipped to my mouth at the sick-ening crunch of my dad's shoulder ramming against the corner of a white lab bench. As they continued to fight, I scrambled to reach the death ray, but the barrel hung at an odd, broken angle. It was useless.

"Sir!" A voice came from a small radio on Nolan's shoul-der. We weren't the only ones wired for communication.

"Sir!" the voice repeated. "You better get out of there! The police are here and they're demanding to speak to you."

Martha had done it! The jolt of happiness hit me all at once. We could still corner Nolan! We just needed to stall him long enough for the police to arrest him.

Nolan screamed with fury. He shoved Dad to the ground and stood up, wiping his bleeding lip with his palm. A smear of red stained the side of his face. Beneath him, Dad didn't stir. Pickles dug her claws into my arm and wound her way around my neck.

"Sorry, Nikki," he said. "That's my cue." He stepped over Dad. Removing his ripped suit jacket, Nolan straightened the bloody collar of shirt and looked me in the eye. A red welt had started to bloom on his temple. "If you ever want to work with someone who recog-nizes your talent, let me know. You deserve better than this guy." He winked at me. "Hope to see you again soon."

I was too mad to think straight. Reaching up to Pickles, I tore the ring from her collar and squeezed it in my palm. Nolan still hadn't realized that I had it, probably because he assumed Dad would never let me even handle it. He'd underestimated Dad again. If I was going to use the element of surprise against him, it had to be now.

I wanted nothing more than to attack him, but seeing Dad on the floor and Leo straining but failing to get to his feet jerked me back to reality. Nolan was much bigger and stronger than I was. Plus, he had a ring of his own and months or years more practice with it than I'd had.

As much as I longed to become some kind of monster to defeat him, I couldn't risk it. Not with Dad and Leo both needing help.

I released my grip and pocketed the ring as Nolan turned on his heel and disappeared.

Dad seemed to be in the most pain. But even though Nolan had gotten away, I couldn't help feeling lucky: Dad was still alive. We were *all* still alive.

"Dad!" I said. I tried to gently shake his hand to get his attention. "Can you hear me? How many fingers am I holding up?"

"Nikki," he mumbled. He shoved himself up onto his elbow and stopped quickly, reeling with dizziness.

"The police are outside." The wound above his right eye was bleeding heavily, but it didn't look too deep. I gently dabbed some of the blood with my sleeve. "Martha told them everything."

He shook his head. "Is Leo okay?"

I found Leo, who was still catching his breath by the door. "He'll be all right," I confirmed. "He got shoved is all."

Dad's eyes fluttered closed for a moment. He probably had a concussion, and I knew that you should never let someone fall asleep after a head injury. Dad needed medical attention, and fast.

"Come on." I shook him gently. "Let's get out of here. You need a doctor."

He shook his head again. "I have to go after Nolan," he said. "He won't leave us be after this."

"Dad, you can barely stand up."

"Doesn't . . . matter . . ." He tried again to right himself but toppled pitifully back to the floor. A trickle of red weaved its way down the side of his face. I could tell by the way his arm sat that his shoulder could be dislocated.

Was it true? With Nolan in the picture, we would never truly be safe again. I tried to imagine what my life would have been like without Nolan lurking in the background. Dad would have been able to stay with us. On that evening seven years ago, he would have come home to tell me another bedtime story.

I would have had a real dad all these years.

There was only one choice left. "I'm going to stop him."

Dad grabbed my arm. "No, Nikki," he said. His words were slurred, but I could still make them out. "Nolan is too dangerous. This isn't some action movie where the good guys always win. He won't hesitate to hurt you. We're lucky he didn't realize your ferret brought the ring to us. And we do have one consolation prize . . ."

I blinked at him. "What's that?"

He held up a shaky hand, showing me a small memory stick. "Is that his?" I gasped. "That's all the research!"

A hint of satisfaction crossed over Dad's face. "I need you two to do me a favor."

"We can talk about favors after we get you a doctor," I said, wiping another trickle of blood from his eyebrow.

"No, this is important." He grabbed my hand and put the memory stick in my palm, wrapping my fingers around it. "I need you and Leo to get this to Martha and the police, okay?"

"What?" Leo cut in. "You're not coming with us?"

Dad gripped my elbow for support and struggled to his feet. "I'll be right behind you," he promised. "But this is the last time I'll ever be in this laboratory. There's important work—research of my own—here. There might be something we can use against him in the future. I'm sure we haven't seen the last of him."

I licked my lips, tasting salt. "I don't want to leave you here. This place freaks me out."

Dad huffed out a weak laugh, and his glance darted to the door. "He's long gone, Nikki. But you two really need to hurry. Get that research straight to Martha. Don't stop for anything. She'll know what to do with it. The authorities need to know what he's been up to."

"He's right," Leo said gently. "Nolan could realize any minute that we've got his memory stick." He touched my hand.

I swallowed down the crushing feeling and nodded. We'd lost this one. Getting Nolan's research to Martha would be better than nothing.

But saving the world from his ring? We'd have to do that another day.

"We'll meet you downstairs," I said, defeated. "But if you're not there in five minutes, I'm coming right back up."

Dad smiled. His eyes looked clearer now—his dizziness was waning. "Just get to Martha," he said. "I'll see you soon." He gave my shoulder a squeeze, and then Leo and I rushed out the door.

We wasted no time finding the rest of our team. I'd never been so happy to see the others as I was when we reached the main entrance. The police had formed a barricade outside the building. A tiny glimmer of hope grew inside me. There was no way Nolan would be able to find his way past the authorities.

Unless . . .

The crescent moon above us caught my attention. Stars were beginning to sparkle in the night sky, and the red and blue lights on top of the police cars danced with them, sending their beams all the way to the rooftops.

The police rushed us, but once they realized we were kids, they let us pass without question and shuffled us to the paramedics, who checked for injuries. Kids

couldn't wield dangerous inventions or be genius scientists, right?

If they only knew.

Once the paramedics finished, Grace waved us over. Charlie was her human self again, and Mo, Bert, and Martha bounced with anticipation for us to join them. But the best sight? Mary, still in one piece! Tears filled my eyes as I rushed over to give her a hug.

"I'm so glad you're all right!" Mary exclaimed.

"That *I'm* all right?!" I sputtered, holding her by the shoulders to check her over. Thankfully, she looked downright normal. Hadn't she just been taken hostage by dangerous criminals? "You're the one who got kid-napped! I'm so sorry, Mary." I gulped and hugged her again.

She tucked a rogue lock of frizzy hair behind her ear. "Please. I never doubted for a second that you guys would rescue me. Besides, you promised me during our last life-or-death simulation that you'd make me your top priority. Right?" She fake-glared at me and giggled.

"That's true." I sighed. "You can always count on me. But why on earth would you tell them you knew some-thing about the ring?! You could have been killed, Mary." I clamped my mouth shut after saying it, worried I'd jinx the good fortune that had kept her safe.

"I told her the same thing." In her usual fashion, Martha had snuck up beside us like an invisible cat. She stretched her arm out to give me a brief hug. "I'm happy to see you safe and sound, too, Nikki."

Seeing Martha out of her usual environment was weird, but my spirits lifted just to have her nearby. This was the first time she'd flown in on a mission since I'd joined the Academy, and hearing her calm, collected voice was like getting a pep talk without all the cheesy mantras.

"Oh!" I remembered Dad's instructions. I handed her the small memory stick he'd given me. "This is for you." I presented it with a little flourish. "It's Nolan's research. Dad stole it off him when they were fighting."

She took the memory stick and turned it over in her palm. Bert, who had been chatting with Leo a few feet away, did a double take and trotted over to us.

"Hey!" he said, pointing to me. "Did Mike give that to you? Those are my plans for the fireworks—Mike wanted to borrow the research to check out and . . ." His mouth dropped open as he noticed the look on my face. "*Annnd* I've said something wrong, haven't I? You don't mind that I shared it with him, do you?"

"Fireworks?" I shook my head. He had to be mistaken. "Dad got this from Nolan directly. They fought and he stole it."

My skin began to prickle.

Bert pinched his lips together. "*No,*" he said. "Sorry, Nik, but this is my memory stick. Look." He grabbed it from Martha and flipped it over, showing me the small *BE* monogrammed in silver.

Bert Einstein.

Beside him, the color drained from Leo's face.

My head snapped back toward the building. I replayed the events in the lab, desperate to find a loophole that meant Dad hadn't lied, that he was taking his time getting back to us. There had to be some mistake, some miscommunication. He should really be out of there by now . . .

I could still feel his hand on my shoulder, giving it a squeeze of support before he'd taken off. What had he said to us?

I'll be right behind you.

The exact same thing I'd said to Leo when I wanted to keep him away from Nolan.

"Oh no . . . He tricked me," I said. The realization tightened around my heart like a fist. "He went after Nolan."

I looked up at the roof of the building, angry tears pricking at the back of my eyes. Remember what I said earlier about life sometimes giving you a win? Forget I ever mentioned that. Sometimes life likes to be a total jerk.

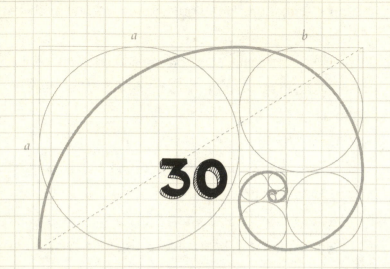

30

"I have to help him." I started to run for the door, but Martha had fast reflexes. She caught me by the elbow with an iron grip.

"The building is still being secured, Nikki," she said in an even tone. "There is no way the police will allow you inside now that you're out. They've got a barricade up." She was trying to calm me down, but with every second that ticked by, the fear and anxiety over Dad's safety choked me more and more. He was in there facing Nolan *alone*. Why hadn't he let me help him?

One of our last conversations came crashing back to me. What had I promised him? To make a run for it if things got out of control?

No.

I'd promised that I would abandon the plan if I calculated there was *zero* chance of us succeeding. If the odds were too stacked against us. If I saw no way for us to beat Nolan.

Is that where we were? *Was* there no way to for us to beat him?

I'd thought it was all over, but Dad didn't seem to think so. He was still up there, looking for a way to save us all.

He thought there was still a chance, or else he wouldn't have lied to us and gone after Nolan.

"I don't care about the barricade!" I glanced at the cluster of police officers, still surveying the building. I didn't need Martha's empty words. I needed *action*. I caught Leo's attention. "Please. I have to get in there. *Do something* so I can go help him."

Leo frowned, but he didn't miss my meaning. He glanced to our right, where a distracted officer had left his police cruiser's door gently ajar.

Catching his eye once more, I let my torso collapse, dropped my face into my hands, and began to sob loudly. To anyone watching, I was a devastated bystander, upset about her father. But what I really needed was to dislodge Martha's hand from my elbow. I could only hope I was as good at this as Mo had been.

"I'm deeply sorry, Nikki, but in this situation, with such a police presence, I'm afraid there's no safe way to—" Martha began.

The police cruiser's blaring horn interrupted her. Every head in the crowd jerked abruptly to the car, which now flashed a circus of lights and siren noises in chaotic succession. And behind the wheel? Leo, with a delighted look of hysteria on his face. The muted yelling of his own voice was drowned out by the whoops and wails of the car's sirens, but it wasn't hard to spot him in the driver's seat, twisting and air-drumming jerkily like a rock star.

It was the perfect distraction.

I seized the moment and raced toward the door, skidding under the caution tape while the police were otherwise occupied. I needed to act fast. I only had a few seconds before they realized their mistake.

"Nikki, no!" Grace's voice echoed from the other side of the noisy parking lot. She must have realized my plan a second too late. I'd have a *lot* of angry geniuses to reckon with if I made it out of this little stunt alive, but that was a problem for Future Nikki.

Present Nikki had to save Dad.

I shouldered my way through the door and locked it behind me. It wouldn't stop anyone for long, but it would give me a head start. Even the police didn't know what they were up against with Nolan and his ring. Luckily for them, they wouldn't be finding out anytime soon. One quick glimpse out the front windows of the building told me that Leo was now *driving* the cruiser, jerking it forward in slow, screeching lunges. Three police officers pounded on the driver's-side window, hopping and halting alongside as it lurched away from the compound.

"Thank you," I whispered to him. I could only hope to tell him in person when this was all over.

Racing to the stairs, I started the climb. The one place where Nolan would stand a chance at escaping through the police barricade would be the roof; that helipad couldn't have been for show. Dad would know that, too.

Panting and sweating like crazy, I finally made it to the top floor and shoved open a heavy metal door marked "Roof Access." Over an hour ago, we'd all landed here with our parachutes. It was still just as silent, save for the wind in the trees and the mild thump of footsteps on the concrete below.

I crept forward in the dark, thankful for the light of the moon to keep me from tripping. With every step, I searched frantically for any sign of Dad or Nolan. There hadn't been a helicopter on the roof when we'd first parachuted in, but one now sat before me like a huge black cat, ready to pounce.

"Nikki?!"

The hushed sound of Dad's voice made my knees buckle with relief. He was crouched behind a chimney of dark bricks, watching the helicopter. "Why didn't you tell me you were going after Nolan?" I scolded him. "He could have killed you!"

Dad couldn't stop the smug grin from curling his mouth. He must have known I'd try to come back for him—I'm *his* daughter, after all. I inherited half my stubbornness from him.

"You shouldn't be here," he said, mimicking my angry tone. "It's way too dangerous for you!"

I rolled my eyes, ignoring his concerns. If he wasn't giving up, neither was I. "Where is he?"

"At the south side of the roof," Dad said. "Stay down! He's talking on the phone, and I overheard him saying he needed something from his main office. It can't be the ring, since he's already got it on him. But maybe some important files or buyer information?" He shook his head with frustration. "I have no idea . . ."

"How do we stop him?" I asked through gritted teeth. "I don't have a weapon, other than the ring. And I honestly don't trust it to help when Nolan has his own!"

Dad's eyes flashed and he grabbed me by the shoulders. "That's right!" he said. "You've got the ring. Give it to me!"

I forced myself to stay calm, despite the urgency racing in my blood. I understood his thinking, but the vision of my father fighting with Nolan earlier was still lodged in my mind. Nolan was younger and much stronger than Dad. Would Dad stand a chance? I started to reach for the ring in my pocket, but a tiny warning inside me made my arm freeze in midair.

"That won't work!" I said. "We need to outsmart him, not outfight him. I don't want you to get hurt, Dad! Plus, you're already injured." I narrowed my eyes at the stain of blood above his eyebrow. Something about the wound struck me as odd. It had stopped bleeding, which had to be a good sign for him.

Dad frowned and pointed to the helicopter. "I've got it," he said. He still had a hold on my shoulder, like he was afraid I was going to leave without him. "We take his helicopter. That will be two strikes against him: He won't be able to escape, *and* he won't get his hands on my ring so he won't be able to perfect his own. No buyer in his right mind would want technology that hasn't been fully developed. It's our best option."

I chewed my lip. It wasn't exactly a foolproof plan, but it was as good as any we had. "Okay," I said. "But we'd better hurry. His phone call could end at any minute."

We raced over to the helicopter, and Dad began to prepare it for takeoff.

"Are you sure he's over there?" I craned my neck and tried to peer around the corner, but there was no sign of Nolan anywhere. The clammy feeling of being *watched* settled over my skin like a wet blanket. Someone as smart as Nolan should know how important it was to keep an eye on his only means of escape.

Unless he *was* keeping an eye on it.

Was Nolan one step ahead of us again? Spiders of doubt began to creep over me.

"Dad," I murmured, edging toward him. "This doesn't feel right. I think we're missing something. It shouldn't be this easy . . ."

Dad opened the door to the helicopter and whispered back to me, "You're used to things being difficult. Take a win for once."

"I guess you're right." I pivoted around to inspect our surroundings one last time. Even the leaves on the trees seemed to be uncertain, rustling like a shiver up a spine.

"Ready, Nikki?" He extended his hand to me. "Come on, hop in."

I stepped forward and took his hand, but the look in his eyes made me pause. The wound above his left eye had begun to trickle a thin stream of blood over his cheek again.

"This reminds me of all those bedtime stories you used to tell me," I said, keeping my voice light. "When the princess would run away from the castle in the middle of the night . . ."

Dad smiled, waving me forward. "That was one of my favorites, too."

"Yeah." I didn't take my eyes off him. "Too bad you've never read me a princess story in my entire life, huh?" I yanked my hand away, forcing myself to stand tall. Maybe this villain could sense fear.

Dad didn't falter, but the tiniest edge of a smirk flickered on his face.

"Oh dear." His shoulders slumped in false sadness. "Have I ruined the surprise? What gave it away?"

I sneered and pointed to his bleeding eyebrow. "It was the right eyebrow, not the left. Nice try though."

I didn't waste any more time. Bolting away, I raced for the other side of the roof. There was a reason the helicopter had been sitting there, practically begging us to steal it. Nolan hadn't left it unattended at all.

He'd counted on me returning and bringing the ring with me.

And I'd almost fallen for it. Two steps into the helicopter, and he could have flown anywhere in the world with me and his precious ring.

Dad's voice echoed behind me. He wasn't freaking out or even mad. Instead, there was a triumphant tone behind his words. "There's nowhere to go, Nikki. But I meant what I said! We can both leave this place in one piece. I'll even give you your dad's cut of the profits! I know you've got some great ideas. Let's work together!"

I tried to put as much distance between myself and that voice as I possibly could, surging forward until I found what I was looking for. Unfortunately, Nolan was faster than me and had circled around the opposite side of the roof to cut me off. I skidded to a stop, the soles of my shoes screeching on the rooftop.

Dad beamed at me and held his arms wide, like he was waiting for a hug. "I knew you'd come back. You seemed stubborn from the start. Hard to leave your ol' dad behind after all this time, right?"

I backed away from him, desperation forcing the air

from my lungs. But no matter how awful or terrifying he was, I knew I couldn't leave.

Beside him, tied up in a rusty chair with a gag over his mouth, was *another* Dad. *My* Dad.

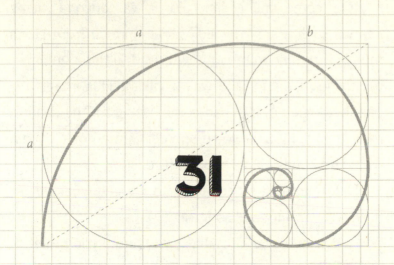

The two Dads stared at me, waiting for my next move.

I racked my brain for a solution to this terrifying equation. How could I have been so *stupid*?! Of *all* the things Nolan could have transformed into, why would he pick my own father?!

Of course, I knew the answer. Turning into my dad was the only way I'd ever leave with him, and since I had the ring with me, he could wipe out his competition and—handy bonus—terrorize my father by kidnapping me in one fell swoop. But I couldn't let him get away with it. I raced forward to help Dad, but Nolan stopped me.

"I seriously do not like you." My mouth curled in disgust.

"Oh, come on," Nolan said. It was beyond freaky hearing such a smarmy, edgy tone coming from Dad's mouth. It reminded me of how I used to think of him— back when I thought he was a villain. This imaginary, parallel version of him had come back from the dead to haunt me. "I thought you'd appreciate the irony." Nolan rested his hands on his hips, relaxed.

Dad mumbled something into his gag, shaking his head while trying to dislodge it.

"It's going to be all right," I told him. I tried to send him telepathic messages that I had a plan.

Of course, I was totally lying. I had no idea how I was going to get out of this one. But I wasn't about to let Nolan know it. Fake it till you make it was my only option.

"Is that so?" Nolan asked. He circled Dad like a shark, taking slow, deliberate steps. "Because from my point of view, things are looking a little dire for you. You're going to give me the ring, or your father is going to suffer the consequences."

He started pushing Dad's chair closer to the edge of the rooftop, sending my stomach twisting with dread. Dad desperately dragged his boots against the rough concrete, but it was no use. Scenes from the past began to flash through my mind. Dad reading to me at bedtime.

Dad helping me design experiments. Making my lunches
and drawing cartoon rocket ships and singing silly songs
about my first inventions.

I'd spent years hating him for what I thought he was,
and now it was time to show him how sorry *I* was. For
doubting him. For not once looking past the gossip to
find the real truth.

"No!" I stomped my foot down. "Stop! I'll give you
the ring!"

Nolan froze. Dad's face was as pale as the moon. He shook his head back and forth, urging me to change my mind. But there was no other way.

I wouldn't lose him again, even if it meant giving up on everything else.

"No tricks," Nolan said. It wasn't a question. His eyes closed, and his skin began to bubble and shift. He was even faster than Dad had been at his transformations. Within seconds, the real Nolan stood before me. As the evil version of Dad disappeared from Nolan's face, I knew he was gone forever in my heart, too. The greedy man who had abandoned his family had never really existed.

"No tricks," I assured Nolan. "I'll give you the ring. You can sell both prototypes for billions and never hear from us again. Just don't hurt him, please."

Nolan held out his hand to me. "Good girl."

I ignored the sharp pang of panic in my chest and dug into my pocket. Pulling out the ring, I eyed Dad one more time. He held his breath, and I knew he must be hoping that I would save his life *and* chuck the ring from the rooftop in equal parts. If I were in his position, I would hate to watch Nolan get away with this.

But I couldn't risk it. Nothing was worth as much to me as Dad's life.

I handed the ring to Nolan, who stuck it onto his ring finger. Two glittering silver rings now adorned his hand, and a satisfied grin spread across his face.

"I knew you were more reasonable than your father," he said. "And no hard feelings about the last seven years either." There wasn't a trace of remorse on his face. "You were better off without him."

Here's the thing: If Nolan had shut up and gone on his way, leaving Dad and I behind, the whole mission probably would have ended there. He would have had both rings, made gazillions of dollars, and we would have had to watch our backs for the rest of our lives as he lurked around in the shadows.

But he had to go and insult my dad.

Fiery heat grew in my chest and my ears began to burn. A burst of angry adrenaline surged through my bloodstream. *What did you say?*

Nolan gave me a pitying look. "I said you were better off without him." He seemed to enjoy taunting me. A vicious gleam shone in his eyes, followed by a softened gaze. "My offer still stands. If I can't have Mike on my team, I'll gladly take his daughter. I'm sure he'd *love* that. Wouldn't you?" Nolan grinned at Dad, who had slumped down in his chair now that exhaustion and defeat had caught up with him.

Honestly, why did evil geniuses keep asking me to work with them? Do I have some sign on my forehead that says "Will Work for Villains"?

But something else was happening, too. Parts of Nolan's body had begun to flicker in and out of existence, like the glitching screen of a buffering video game. His ears shrunk down into much smaller versions of themselves, then swelled back again. His hair, already sweaty and disheveled, became darker and distinctly more *fur-like* before blinking back to normal.

Then three very surprising things happened all at once: First, a sharp crack split the air—one of Bert's firecrackers, it sounded like—and a burst of thick gray smoke appeared behind us.

Second, a lone figure dashed out from around the corner, his sneakers skidding on the damp rooftop. *Leo!* He made a break for Dad, shoving him out of Nolan's reach and clawing at the ropes that bound him to the chair.

Third, Leo reminded me of two words that I hadn't thought about since our time in Dad's volcano laboratory. "Cellular memories!" he bellowed, frantically unknotting the ropes around Dad. "The ring remembers you, Nikki! *Concentrate!*"

Cellular memories.

That's right!

Warmth radiated through me, and my heart began to drum. *Leo had figured it out.* Nolan wasn't in control of his body's weird flickering and shifting . . .

I was.

The ring not only remembered me but it was picking up on my exceedingly heightened emotions. And no matter who this guy was, he was no match for my dad in the brains department. Dad's ring would be more powerful than anything Nolan could invent.

And my anger was more powerful than anything he could feel.

Now that Dad's ring was on Nolan's finger, I could use it against him.

We still had a chance.

Only a few seconds had passed since Leo's arrival, but all the clouds in my brain had cleared out of the way, revealing the sun. Only it wasn't a sun pouring out of me, it was a supernova—vicious and focused. I let myself feel everything I'd been running from. The dinners I'd endured without Dad. The anxiety that I'd turn out just like him. The emptiness when I'd realized I'd been hating him for nothing. On the inside I was throwing glass, screaming in a fit of rage, kicking and punching walls— *anything* to let the fury free. Seven years of hurt funneled into one white-hot beam of anger, sadness, resentment, and pain.

Only instead of aiming it at Dad, I aimed it at the man who had been behind all of it.

And I knew *exactly* what I wanted Nolan to become.

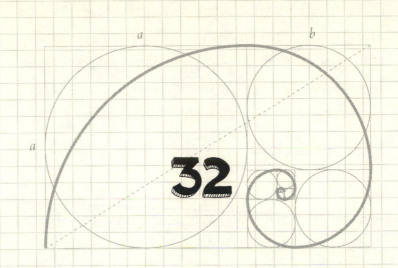

32

Though he tried to fight it, I was right: Nolan's prototype was no match for Dad's ring or my anger. They say there's no fury like a woman scorned, right? Well, try a ticked-off tween with seven years of anger stored up and nothing left to lose.

I focused all my energy onto the ring, urging it to listen to me. A crushing pressure in my head grew until I could barely stand it. Then, suddenly, the mental strain eased the tiniest bit. It felt like someone was lending me a hand. But how? I didn't need to tear my eyes away from Nolan to know what was happening: Dad was *helping* me, willing the ring he'd invented to listen to *us* and not Nolan.

A wave of power surged through me. We could do this together.

First, Nolan's ears began to flicker again. Then his nose glitched between flesh and fur. Nolan eyes flashed with curious recognition—he was starting to put together what was happening. All those years ago, his biggest mistake was underestimating our family, and now he was going to lose by doing the same thing.

He tried to pull Dad's ring from his finger, but as he realized he was too late, his face twisted in confusion. Then, in one quick blip that sent a crack of smoke through the air, he shrank down in front of us and landed on four paws. Two silver rings clanged down beside him, tumbling across the dirty concrete toward my feet. A memory stick, mangled and bloody, settled beside them.

Dr. Nolan was no more.

Leo was at my side within seconds. "A ferret?!" He darted forward and grabbed Nolan by the scruff of the neck, before he could scurry away. Nolan, absolutely livid at this turn of events, attempted to scratch Leo's arms, but Leo's grip was too tight. "How did you get the rings off him?!"

I pressed my hand to my forehead. Turns out that projecting seven years' worth of anger onto your nemesis can give you a bit of a migraine. "I wanted him to be a harmless ferret, and to get the rings far away from him so he couldn't hurt us anymore. It looks like Dad's ring—the one that can respond to my thoughts—took that into account. But I think we have Dad to thank for the memory stick." I had to lean forward and rest my hands on my knees to catch my breath.

Leo held the ferret up for inspection. Nolan's beady black eyes glared daggers back at us. "He's not talking," he mused. "Shouldn't he be able to talk?"

I made a face. "Yeah, I wanted him to shut up, too. He's done enough talking. Now he's a mute ferret."

I grabbed both rings and Nolan's memory stick and stuffed them into my pocket, then hobbled over to Dad. He was freeing the last of the ropes from his legs and tossing them aside.

"You two should never have come back," he scolded me while pulling me in for a hug so tight I could barely breathe. "It was dangerous. Reckless. Completely irresponsible." He shook his head, talking into my hair.

I let out an exhausted breath. "And . . . ?"

"And exactly what I would have done," he admitted, releasing me. He patted Leo on the shoulder. "That was quick thinking with the fireworks. Thank you."

"No problem, sir." Leo grinned his perfect lopsided smile. "Hey, would you mind taking him?" He held out the squirming ferret in one hand. "I think we should probably get Nolan down to Martha before he bites someone. He could have rabies for all we know."

I giggled at the ferret's indignant face. "I don't think he's too happy to be a rodent," I said, poking him in the belly.

"Mustelid," Leo and Dad said in unison.

"I'll take him," Dad said. "I want to get him in custody before he has a chance to scurry off. He's useless as a ferret, but there's no way I'm taking my eyes off him until he's locked up. And I want both of you checked out by the paramedics. Understood?"

"Yes, Daaad," I intoned, rolling my eyes.

"Ready, Nikki?" Leo grabbed my hand, and together we followed my father as he limped toward the roof's exit.

I laced my fingers through his. "Our friends aren't going to be happy with either of us, you know," I said. "How did you even get up here? Last I looked, you were in that police cruiser causing a scene . . ."

He winced. "I might have driven it around the back of the building and into a tree. Bert and Mo set off a few more fireworks, and I used the diversion to sneak in the back into the stairwell."

"You knew that Nolan had the ring—what were you even thinking?"

"You'd have done the same for me. I couldn't stand the thought of anyone threatening you forever." He shrugged. "Besides, everyone's going to be more ticked off at *you* for coming up here alone in the first place."

"Maybe we should take the helicopter and get out of here. Let Grace cool down for a while," I suggested.

Leo beamed. "Where's the fun in that? And one more thing, Nikki . . . ?" He stopped in his tracks in front of the door. Dad's muted footsteps continued to echo lightly down the staircase.

"What?"

"Remind me never to tick you off," he whispered.

And that, dear reader, was the only moment of the day that I truly hadn't anticipated. I'd expected that I might die, or be defeated by Nolan, or lose my cookies skydiving with Dad.

But I hadn't expected Leo to *kiss me*.

Yes—you read that right!

Right there, on the rooftop, with the police waiting below us and my dad just a few steps away with a furious enemy-turned-ferret in his hand, Leo tucked a curl of messy hair behind my ear and gave me my first kiss.

Now, I know that the whole space-time continuum is still under debate, but I will say this: If there *is* any way to time travel, I bet scientists will find the answer is kissing. I'm not sure if ours lasted two seconds or two minutes. Maybe it was two years? All I know is that in that moment, I forgot about everything. There were no equations. No disasters. The entire world seemed to melt away, leaving just Leo and me, on a rooftop under the moon.

I even forgot about the stupid ferret that had just tried to kill us all.

"Uh, *excuse me*?"

We both leaped apart at the sound. I knew I looked guilty, red-faced, and dopey. But Leo, to my surprise, had a mellow look of perky contentment on his face. Somehow it made him even more adorable.

"'Sup, guys?" Leo said brightly.

"Well now, I hope our attempts to save your life aren't *interrupting* anything!" Bert stood before us, his eyes bulging. He wore the gloves I'd used to scale the ship in the Galápagos. Behind him, Grace, Mary, Charlie, and Mo had their hands on their hips, and a bundle of tied

parachutes rested at Mary's feet. Pickles wound herself around Grace's shoulder, and even she was giving me a ferrety look that said, *"Oh no you didn't!"*

Dad's footsteps sounded behind the door, and he stepped back out onto the roof, clearly wondering what was taking us so long. "Are you guys coming or— Oh, hey, everyone! Glad to see that you're all okay!" He gave them a little wave, ensuring that Nolan the ferret was still tightly gripped in his hand.

"Yeah, hi!" My voice was traitorously hoarse and my mind blanked. "Uh...How did you guys get up here?!" I pinched my lips together. Maybe if I made them disappear, I could make it seem like they hadn't seen anything. But judging by the look on Mary's face—a playful "I told you so" kind of look—they weren't about to be fooled.

"What...?" Dad said, blinking with confusion. "Did I miss something?"

I stared at my feet while Mary stifled a sharp giggle.

"How did *we* get up here?" Bert repeated, incredulous. He adjusted his glasses and pointed to the furry ball of fury in Dad's hand. "Who's the ferret?!"

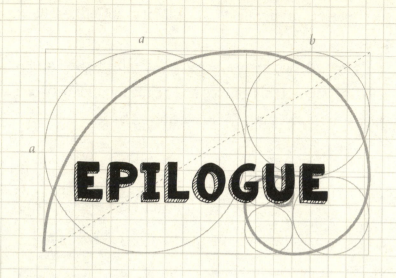

EPILOGUE

The familiar house flanked with trees sent a happy rush of excitement through me. It had been a couple of months since I'd seen it, and the crisp fall air and a cozy trail of smoke coming from the fireplace made anything seem possible.

Hopefully, anything *was* possible.

"Don't just stand there," I said. "One knock, and we get this over with. Aren't you curious to see what happens?"

Dad stopped with his hand in midair in front of the door. His shoulder was wrapped in a sling, a single flower tucked into it by his wrist. We'd been standing there for at least five minutes already, and the autumn chill was starting to make my nose run. I could smell

the crisp, woodsy scent of turning leaves. Change was in the air.

"I don't know, Nikki," he said. He let his hand drop again to his side. "Do you think she'll even hear me out?"

I glanced back at the Academy van, where my friends

were waiting. "Go!" Grace mouthed in the passenger side window. Charlie and Mary clapped their hands soundlessly behind the side window. Bert and Leo gave us both a thumbs-up from the back seat, eager to show their support.

"You got this, Mike!" Leo hollered.

"I've tried every equation I can think of," I said. "And the truth is, I have no idea how Mom's going to react. But there's only one way to find out."

"Right," he said. "Sometimes you need to try something to see if it will work. Let's do this."

He stood taller and straightened out his jacket and tie. He'd gotten a fresh haircut for the occasion, and without the threat of global disaster looming over him, he looked a lot like I remembered him, all those years ago.

"Together," I said, lifting my hand to join his. "One, two . . ."

We both knocked on the door.

To Be Continued

AUTHOR'S NOTE

All of the characters and events in this book are fictional, yet they are based on some real-life people who have had incredible adventures in human history. You may already be familiar with Nikola Tesla (for whom Nikki is named!), as well as the other students at Genius Academy and their real life historical counterparts. But have you ever heard of Michael Faraday?

Michael Faraday was born on September 22, 1791. While they were not related like Nikki and her dad, Faraday was a huge influence on Tesla. Unlike some scientists, Faraday was completely self-taught. At age fourteen, he worked as an apprentice to a bookbinder and found himself very curious about the books he was making. He didn't want to *make* books—he wanted to *read* them and learn everything he could. He stayed late at work to read and, eventually, used his knowledge to become an assistant to a local chemist, despite having no formal science education.

Fast-forward through a lot of lectures, experiments, long days, and hard work, and today Faraday is known as one of the founders of electrochemistry. He discovered electric induction: the premise that if you move a magnet through a metal loop, the metal loop will have an electric current running through it. He used this knowledge to invent the first transformer and the first electric generator. These inventions set the stage for all modern transformers, generators, and motors. He also had several inventions and scientific principles named after him, including the Faraday cage, Faraday paradox, and Faraday's law of induction, among others.

But Michael Faraday wasn't just a genius scientist who changed the world with his knowledge and inventions. He was also the founder of the Royal Institution's "Christmas Lectures," a special program to introduce science education to children. This series has continued since 1825, pausing only briefly during World War II. Its lectures sparked an interest in science for millions of children, and I have no doubt that he would enjoy the chance to reach new readers and future scientists today.

To learn more about Michael Faraday, or any of the historical geniuses that inspired the Elements of Genius series, visit your local school or public library.

ACKNOWLEDGMENTS

Whoa! You're reading the acknowledgments! When I was younger, I loved reading the acknowledgments, too. (In fact, I still do!) It always felt like a magical peek behind the real life of a book, and all the incredible people it took to make it. It might be my name on the cover, but you know the truth: It takes many people to make a book and even more to get it into your hands! This book belongs to you, and it belongs to everyone listed here.

I will forever be grateful to Kathleen Rushall, Jenne Abramowitz, and Shelly Romero for their support and editorial eyes on this book. Dick Robinson, Abby McAden, Keirsten Geise, Josh Berlowitz, Rachel Feld, Erin Berger, Jordana Kulak, Lizette Serrano, Julia Eisler, Anne Marie Wong, Anne Shone, Diane Kerner, Nikole Kritikos, Lori Grafstein, Stella Grasso, Denise Anderson, and *everyone* in the Scholastic and Scholastic Canada families—it's a joy working with all of you, and your tireless efforts to bring books into the world inspire me every day. Readers, are you curious about the incredible illustrations in this book? You can thank Lissy Marlin for those! (And I will, too—thanks, Lissy!)

Did you notice the quote at the beginning of this book? I started with Mary Oliver, and I think it's fitting to end with her. Mary Oliver (a wonderful American poet) believed that we should always keep room in our hearts for the unimaginable. I want to thank my friends, family, and brilliant readers for always inspiring me to stay curious and keep extra room in my heart for all that magic out there. I hope this book inspires you to look for the magic, too—and maybe even make some of your own!

ABOUT THE AUTHOR

As a zoologist and author, Jess Keating has been sprayed by skunks, bitten by crocodiles, and victim of the dreaded paper cut. Her books blend science, humor, and creativity, and include the acclaimed My Life Is a Zoo middle-grade trilogy and award-winning picture books, like *Shark Lady* and *Pink Is for Blobfish*. Jess lives in Ontario, Canada, where she loves hiking, nerdy documentaries, and writing books for curious and adventurous kids. Jess can be found online at jesskeating.com or on Twitter at @Jess_Keating.